The First Atheist

Eric Polfliet

Llumina Press

Requests for permission to make copies of any part of this work should be mailed to Permissions Department, Llumina Press, PO Box 772246, Coral Springs, FL 33077-2246

ISBN: 1-59526-623-2 PB
      1-59526-625-9 E-book

Printed in the United States of America by Llumina Press

Library of Congress Control Number: 2006907792

"Never believe a book.

Not even the Bible.

Because on the 6th day, God only

created the prime number."

Ad Hoc translation from Peter Verelst's
Het Spieren-Alfabet (*The Alphabet of Muscles*) p. 69

Acknowledgements

With thanks to Internet search engines—they are transforming the definitions of truth and knowledge.

With thanks to the many authors who I did not mention by name that contributed knowingly and unknowingly to these pages. All that is left is duplication.

With thanks to some of the people who will recognize themselves in these pages.

With thanks to (Rose), whose contribution was essential—our bond will never be broken. Once a name is printed, it exists. You understand.

My parents.

Prologue

Bangkok

They storm up the stairs, the rhythmic sounds of their boots tattooing a rhythm of terror—the same symphony of hate I'd heard many times before in movies, when well-organized SS squads picked up Jews dressed in beautiful Hugo Boss uniforms.

I am locked in my apartment, afraid and old; I have no more strength to fight or resist. When they force their way into my apartment, I realize with astonishment that my apartment is surrounded—top, bottom, left, and right—by similar apartments, all filled with people in fear.

Thin walls hide their faces and separate me from them, but not from the sounds of their fornication, running toilets, or petty arguments. No help is expected.

Then I wake up, sweating and tired. Another bad dream.

I am terrified. They will find me, and I will suffer. I write what I have to write now, before my fears consume me. Then, I will try to forget.

There are no big secrets to be revealed, no fingers to be pointed, no dangerous individuals clearly identified, and no provable conspiracy, only the sad realization that in a stunning reversal of tolerance, people who defend religious ideas with vigor and fanaticism cost lives—every day, every minute. How did we get here?

Where is the tolerant face of religion, thought, and culture? When did we lose this most human capacity—laughter in the face of those who profess to own truth and certainty? When did we lose the capacity for defiant denial in the face of those who claim to know? Is certainty all we want? Finite answers? An easy manual by which to live our daily lives?

Everybody claims righteousness. They will defend their truth, decimating opposing opinions. This work is about an opinion that originated a couple thousand years ago, with a man called Charvaka. To some he was a philosopher, to others a philanderer, to still others a false prophet. He dared to question, but he also liked to drink and have sex. Just mentioning his name was and is enough to draw hate and disgust. He was wiped from the pages of history in one of the oldest and richest cultures in the world.

A girl died trying to keep Charvaka's legacy alive—my girlfriend, the only woman I ever loved. She is always on my mind, both for who she was and the way she died. She now exists only in my memory. A life together would likely have ended in the disaster most marriages do.

These are really the last words I will ever write. I will send them to a journalist-editor—a friend of mine. These pages contain insights I have gathered over the years from diverse sources and people. It does not make for coherent reading; some is true, some of it I think is true. Some I experienced; some just came to me. They took offense.

They wiped Charvaka from the pages of history; they tried to erase me. Now they want to suppress you—your desires, dreams, life. They want you to live piously, in fear of their big boots. And they will make rules, more rules, and give us more things to fear.

Chapter 1

Catholic University of
Leuven, Van Even Road

Belgium, 1981

L euven, where I spent five years at the university. Just before graduation, I left town and never looked back. The events of 1981 triggered a number of experiences that would, twenty-five years later, receive context, but no clarification. An epic struggle has been waged since the beginning of time—no winners, no losers—just victims. In one form or another, we have all played a role in this struggle by the choices we make, the temptations we follow, and the experiences we deny ourselves.

I spent my time in Leuven mainly on Van Even Road, where the faculty of social sciences was based. It was the beginning of the eighties; the social sciences, which had attracted many students in the prior two decades, were losing popularity quickly. The mediocre academic efforts put forth by me and my fellow students certainly did not help. Democracy had done a lot for the number of students that could attend university, but the university had lost sight of its search for excellence.

I spent most of my time with friends in a place called t'STUC, a nonprofit organization that set up cultural events at democratic prices. It was next to the auditorium where I attended courses, and the drinks were cheap. They also served big sandwiches with a lot of red meat at low prices.

My fellow students wore their hair down to their shoulders and listened to what they called "progressive rock"—long, winding songs by musicians in love with themselves and recovering from too many LSD trips. The conversations varied from the political and musical to the utterly mundane: Is Leninism or Trotskyism the real embodiment of the Marxist revolution? Did you read about those punks in England that seem to endorse destruction as their creed? What is their political agenda? Will Hoegaarden ever be a popular beer? Pina Bausch and Anne Teresa De Keersmaeker propelled modern dance to the forefront of the cultural scene and confused those of us who looked for political and social relevance in watching people sit in contortionist poses.

How could I have missed the importance of that day? It was just another lecture covering Indian religions. Was I intellectually lazy? Had my Catholic education strangled me so much that I refused to see the connections? Was I just too young to feel it? Did I not care? I just remember blood—deep, red blood stuck to Persian carpets and exotic clothes. She lay naked with her legs spread wide, her head bashed in by the large stone still lodged in her skull. A thick coat of paint covered her body: her belly, her throat, her forehead, around her vagina. And what was that grass doing around her thighs? What were all these strange signs on the wall? It was so sick…my life changed. Forever.

In those days, it was hard for me to talk to a woman. Chronic shyness and a Catholic-ingrained distrust for the opposite gender had me utterly fucked up. Whenever I slept with a girl, I was overcome with guilt, and social ineptitude kept me from building anything resembling a relationship. But what the hell. Intellectual development was the goal; the rest would follow. So we filled our heads with Hegel, Marx, and the liberation theology so revered in this Catholic bastion. It was the latest gimmick to make the Bible relevant and liberate the South American peasant in one intellectually Olympian effort. God's newest guidebook to a happy life! No way could any of us miss our destiny. We had a task to fulfill. We had God on our side.

Then she came along. The rest lost importance. I saw purpose. Her dark, exotic skin attracted me immediately. I fell in love with Parvati's passion and the amazing nights we had together. Five months later, she was dead, murdered under bizarre circumstances. I never really loved again. I struggled from relationship to relationship, trying to build something that vaguely resembled what I had had with her. My relationship with Parvati never played on a spiritual level; we never talked a lot, we just had a lot of sex. She was experienced. Hardly twenty, yet she taught me to experiment and do things my Catholic background never would have allowed me to do. I was very naïve in those days and thought all women had this knowledge. I learned over the years that this was not so. No woman ever held my attention after Parvati. What was a woman to do with me? I demanded so much. I needed passion. They could not help but fail in comparison to her. When she died, in what looked like a sick, erotic ritual, I never forgot that she liberated me—gave me a sense of power, passion, and desire.

The police were puzzled by her bizarre death. Comparisons with the Manson murders were made. *You know these foreigners—their drugs, their weird habits—then they go too far.*

The Catholic press was outraged; right-wing elements called for a ban on foreign students. I was alone with my pain and desire. Soon after, I left Leuven, and then Belgium. I never returned. I visited once, to put my mother in her final resting place.

Why did we go to the lecture that night? Why was Parvati dead the next morning? I never questioned Parvati's loyalty to me. I never doubted it, even after her body was found following what looked like a sexual orgy as deviant as one could imagine. In five months, she had given me a sense of celebration of our bodies, far beyond the arbitrary restrictions of a monogamous relationship. However, how she made me feel is not the reason I am writing any of this. It took me twenty-five years to understand that our sexual bliss was a celebration far beyond the union of two people with a strong physical attraction to each other. It was an act of defiance, a confirmation of another choice, the actualization of another way of life—free of moral judgments, ignorant of accepted truths, blasphemous for those who read different books.

Chapter 2

Khar Station:
A Jain Holy Man

Bombay, 1993

B ombay, home to twelve million, was still called
Bombay in 1993.

It was only later that the Shiv Sena changed Bombay's
name to Mumbai, in a futile attempt to eradicate any recol-
lection of the British Raj. The Shiv Sena was a political
party named after a 17th century chieftain with liberal and
tolerant credentials, qualities that would be hard to square
with the Shiv Sena's political objectives today.

The Shiv Sainiks (Shiv Sena party members) are or-
dinary Indian citizens: tuk-tuk drivers, sellers of naan
bread, road workers, accountants, police officers, doc-
tors, managers, men, women, and children. They change
occasionally and dress as saffron-clothed warriors—

embodiments of old ghosts, reliving dreams of a greater Hindu state.

At regular intervals, they wreaked havoc in the streets of Bombay, waging war against the Muslim threat or any other threat they perceived—the Enron power plant, Coca-Cola, movies that did not respect Hindu traditions. In this way, they hoped to revive their glorious past. These proud Aryans were led by their guru—a dictator, a demagogue, but according to newspapers, an utterly charming man—Bal Thackery, protector of their Hindu heritage. With his great square glasses, his penchant for stressing his Aryan descent, and a picture of Hitler in his house, he personified India's conundrum as much as anyone did. India, partly sacred—the source of some of the most profound insights in human history—and partly an incredibly cruel society with utter disrespect for other beings (except cattle), was justified by a complex web of religious threats leading back to writings that some claim are the oldest in the world and contain all knowledge: the *Vedas*.

The more the newspapers painted the Shiv Sainiks as a group of thugs, the more political leverage Bal Thackery seemed to gain. Hindustan would be the new name for India. "We are, after all, a Hindu nation," they kept repeating, like one of the bad Banghra raps so popular in the discos along Juhu beach. It was rumored that Bal Thackery's son owned one of the more popular discos. The 180 million Muslims living within the borders of "Hindustan" were not mentioned. The Shiv Sena turned Bombay's multicultural foundation into a bastion unsympathetic to anybody outside the province of Maharastra, but one that mainly despised Muslims.

In 1992, Hindus destroyed the Babri Masjid mosque in Ayodhya, far from Bombay. Muslims believed the temple was a monument to India's first emperor, Babar. According to the Hindus, the Hindu god, Lord Rama, was born there, and a mosque on his birthplace was more than they could bear. Another chapter with more than two thousand dead was added to an ongoing 800-year-old battle. Deadly riots erupted in Bombay. The Shiv Sainiks were implicated; Bal Thackery declared them heroes.

Bombay, however, had more problems. An exploding population meant a chronic housing shortage, a sporadic supply of electricity, and a weak infrastructure. Bombay was severely overpopulated. Everywhere, there were people—twenty-four hours a day. Even when you escaped the oppressive presence of people, you could not escape Bombay, for its smells permeated the air wherever you hid. There was no escape.

On SV Road, Khar, a main shopping area, people literally stepped over each other at improvised market stalls filled with clothes, shoes, household items, gold, and drugs. Most of the items were of very poor quality. It did not matter; the population was so large that anything sold. Quality was not an issue in India's paradise, which was designed by Gandhi and Nehru following their prescription of self-reliance, called *swadeshi*. One day, I bought a can opener. I came home, tried to use it,

9

and it broke into two pieces. I went back to the market stall where I had bought it and asked for a refund.

I never received my refund, but I did receive a lecture on the logic behind Indian economics.

"Why make a can opener that does not break? It would be too expensive. These are the only can openers in India. Good or bad, they will be bought. If you want a good can opener, fly to Singapore or Dubai to get it."

Rats and disease were everywhere. Tuberculosis was rampant, AIDS was exploding before the very eyes of the politicians, but they dealt with it through silence. Silence was the code for survival in the metropolitan madness. How could one deal, day in and day out, with beggars, the crippled, and a corrupt government? The only way was to ignore it, as I did when I lived there, working for a construction company. Oh, sure, the company that employed me sent a hospital bus with a doctor and nurses into a few slums to treat tuberculosis, and they probably cured some people. The cost for our company was minor, but it bought us a wealth of political capital and a lot of peace of mind. Still, many died every day—bad karma.

I remember one event vividly. During my stay in Bombay, the hotel Neelkanth was my home. It was situated on Linking Road, Khar West, one of the northern suburbs of Bombay, not far from Khar station, where my office was based. Every morning, I walked out of the hotel, and my Indian colleague Sony would be waiting for me in a tuk-tuk. Together, we would take our five-minute journey to Khar station. That morning, when I walked across the street, I saw a dark brown man with long, shabby, black hair, and an exposed erect penis sitting on the sidewalk. It was eight in the morning, and buses, cars, and hundreds of pedestrians were walking by. He looked straight into my eyes. There was nothing there—no regret, no madness, no shame, and no loneliness. Nobody looked at him, but every pedestrian saw him; they avoided him carefully and walked in a curved line around him. I stepped into the tuk-tuk with Sony, and we left for work. "The police should lock him up," Sony screamed over the hauling motor of the tuk-tuk.

Brecht said it eloquently. "Erst kommt das Fressen, dann kommt die Moral." First the food, then the morals. With religion littering every aspect of Indian life, and starving people littering every street corner, his adagio took on a very eerie sound. One would have liked to scream it out as a simple solution in this market of misery, where every human disfigurement, mental and physical, was on display. What did one do when one saw children, purposefully maimed, at traffic lights begging for money? What did one do when people with open wounds festering in the sun approached? What did one do when one saw a car hit a person, drive on, and leave the victim lying dead? What did one say about a city where everybody stressed how conservative he or she was, but which has the biggest red-light district in the world? What did one say upon seeing the mutilated faces of women attacked with bottles of acid for not complying with outlawed dowry demands? What did

11

one say about the body of another bride burned in the family oven? Nothing. These are the wrong questions.

Everybody who visits India is confronted with unbelievable paradoxes. Brecht could not solve it. Food is not the answer. When did a full belly ever lead to a better moral being? Morals are never grounded; they change like the wind; they are products of environment and fashion, never universal. Our morals are for sale—wherever you come from, whatever traditions you subscribe to.

Indian TV airs a non-stop dysentery of stories of the Bhagavad-Gita, describing how Lord Krishna convinces the archer Arjuna to do his duty as a warrior and kill friends and family. Doing his duty as a warrior is his moral right.

What does "moral right" mean when we try to liberate ourselves from the cycle of birth? Just as every Catholic wants to go to heaven, every Hindu tries to liberate himself from the circle of birth and rebirth, where one can reappear as an animal or a politician, a beggar or a peasant. It jerks us around like a yoyo on the cosmic waves of karmic faith. We simplified the concept of karma in the West, and we like to believe that doing good deeds gives good karma, ensuring a rebirth with a better social position and a better chance to reach liberation.

It's a good sales pitch to regulate the masses and keep them at bay. Do good, be good, and liberation will follow. It even fits our Christian traditions. Doesn't it feel good when all religions ultimately want the same thing? Or so we are led to believe.

What is not being said is that some respected Hindu teachers do believe that the deeds one does on earth are irrelevant to obtaining liberation. You can go out and kill your family, your neighbors—yet be untouched by sin. Ask Arjuna. India carries this duality in it, and coming from the outside, one can never fully understand. Forget the attempts at rationalization I just gave and respect whatever gets them through the night. They respect what gets us through the night.

Our morals, our religion, and theirs—inventions of repression and good organization. None is better; none is worse. All is acceptable as long as it produces survival and evolution.

Sony was a good man—a Sikh with a big smile and a taste for Johnny Walker Black Label. In those days, bottles of JW were hard to get. I made sure he received a bottle from the duty-free every time a friend flew in from the outside. I say "outside" because this is how you feel once you are in India. There is India and the outside: two worlds with different foods, smells, habits, and laws of gravity—if you believe the stories of flying gurus.

The morning of that fateful day, Sony was excited. He dragged me to the street just around the corner. There was a big, rundown building, the train station of Khar. As usual, different craftsmen were waiting for the foreman, who came to hire men for the day. On the left were the stonecutters; next to them were the metalworkers; next to them were the electricians. You also had a group of people with no specific skill to sell. They were the cheapest. Occasionally, I used some to clean the office where I worked.

That particular morning, there were more people than usual. A lot more. And minute by minute, more people arrived.

"What is going on?" I asked.

"A Jain holy man is coming today."

I did not know what he was talking about.

"A Jain yogi is coming; he took the vow, mahavrata. He walked for 123 days with no food or water."

"But that is impossible—he should be dead."

Sony looked at me with contempt. "He took the great vow; do not doubt that he has unbelievable ascetic stamina."

I was puzzled. Sony, who ran our MIS department with an iron fist and ironclad logic, something instilled in the Catholic colleges of Bombay, did not doubt that a man went without liquid or food for 123 days.

Was he stupid, or what?

Suddenly, the crowd, swollen to a couple of thousand people, started moving like a wave, forward and backward, as if electricity had jolted them. Then he passed by—a naked man—shabby-looking, with a leaf in his hand to protect him against the sun. Monks brushed the ground ahead of where he walked. People all around me tried to touch him. Music blared out of improvised speakers, repeating chants over and over again. It was as if a heat wave had swallowed me; once he passed, everything cooled down. The effect of his passing was so profound I could not ignore it, no more than I could ignore that he was stark naked, his penis swinging like a pendulum from left to right. I asked Sony why he, as a Sikh, was so excited about this naked man. And why should *he* not be arrested?

Chapter 3

Catholic University of Leuven, Ten Minutes from the Van Even Road: A Lecture

Belgium, 1981

*N*ew Age bookshops started springing up in little, cheaply rented houses around the city of Leuven. The books found there covered everything from how to starve one's self with macrobiotic diets and information on Madame Blavatsky and the occult, to how to stop smoking with self-hypnosis. One of these shops, The Other Side, organized a series of lectures on world religions. When they announced a lecture on Hinduism and other religions in India by Professor Kumar, Parvati was hell-bent on going. Professor Kumar was a much respected guest teacher in the philosophy department at the University of Leuven. He was Indian, and he taught at Bombay University.

Until then, I was never conscious of Parvati's different religious background. But one day, when Parvati and I stood in front of a big poster inviting interested parties to the lecture of Professor Kumar, she asked, "Do you know what I mean when I say I am a Hindu?"

"Not really, but you are from India, which is where the Hindu religion comes from, no?"

"But I could have been a Christian, Muslim, Jain, Sikh, Buddhist, or Zoroastrian."

I stood, a bit perplexed, unfamiliar with most of the religions she mentioned, except by name.

"Okay, but you just told me you are a Hindu."

"Hindu is a nationality, not a religion. Did you know that?"

"I honestly did not know. I always thought Hinduism was a religion," I answered, surprised.

"Do you want to know more about the religions in my country?" Parvati asked.

It was a leading question, and I knew it was important to go to Professor Kumar's lecture.

We entered the lecture room in the philosophy department, a ten-minute walk from Van Even Road. The room was traditional of a lecture hall in Leuven—a cone with the lecturer in the center and the listeners surrounding him in horizontal rows that rose steadily toward the back of the room. The philosophy department in Leuven was well respected and had distinguished professors. I had always heard that the writings of the German philosopher Husserl were saved from the Nazis in the

Second World War and were kept somewhere in Leuven in their original form. It is one of the ironies of philosophical history that his protégé, Heidegger, for all his brilliant contributions to philosophy, is remembered for a checkered past and was accused of having collaborated with the Nazis, like many Belgians. This little piece of trivia was of no importance, of course, given the subject of the lecture presented by Professor Kumar that evening.

Professor Kumar walked into the auditorium dressed in a long, white robe, a saffron-colored shawl draped around his neck. He could have just stepped out of a Bollywood production set. A picture-perfect personification of an Indian man, he fulfilled every Western stereotype of how a man from India should look. He started his lecture in a voice faintly touched by English public schools.

"In my youth, my father had a large banyan tree in his garden. Our family gathered under it every Sunday to eat a meal and enjoy each other's company. We often discussed suitable suitors for my sisters, but sometimes my father talked to us about what it meant to be a Hindu."

Parvati's body language changed the moment Professor Kumar started speaking. She was normally a very soft-spoken, gracious person with an enticing smile. She respected others and never tried to antagonize anybody, partly because she was a foreigner, but also because of her culture and family.

We sometimes discussed the aggressive nature of the student protests that often took place in the streets of

Leuven. There was always something to protest, but I do not want to bore you with our causes. Parvati accused me several times of using the protests as a sort of cathartic stress release, for they involved hurling stones at the police without any philosophical foundation. I denied it every time, vehemently, but she was right. She was always so much more mature than I was. So, her sudden outburst at the lecture surprised me enormously.

"A victim of mythology, a slave of Brahmans, justified by undeniable truths, written in a language of discrimination before the word was even invented," Parvati hissed between her teeth, unable to hide the aggressive tremor in her voice.

I looked at her with my finger on my lips, encouraging her to be silent and pay attention to Professor Kumar. Where did that come from? I remember thinking.

"For a Hindu, India is both our ancestral land and the land of our religion," continued Professor Kumar. "We are descendents of the Aryans, who wrote the most important work the world has ever seen, the Vedas. The Vedas contain all knowledge and it is whispered they were received directly from the gods. For a Hindu, the Vedas are the highest authority, not to be questioned by you or me, but devoured with respect and humility. These writings are holy."

"Hey, I heard Billy Graham say the same about the Bible the other day," I whispered in Parvati's ear.

"Who?"

"An American—I'll tell you later."

"Hindus are the indigenous people of India; Hinduism is our indigenous religion—not Islam, not Christianity—their religions did not originate in India."

"Does that mean Muslims and Christians are not Hindus?" I asked Parvati quietly. "You told me before that Hindus were the people of India."

She looked at me, upset. I thought it was because of my question. Later, I realized it was Professor Kumar who was upsetting her.

He continued, "Hinduism is a complicated religion. As I said, the Vedas are the ultimate truth. The Vedas do not have ten commandments; there is no easy prescription for how to live. Hinduism has no founder—no Buddha, no Jesus, no keeper of the truth. The Vedas were written in Sanskrit, an almost dead language, by wise men of great vision, called 'rishis.' Sanskrit is, for us, the language of the gods, capable of expressing eternal truths and profound insights. Sanskrit has a specific poetic quality uniquely placed to express spiritual truths."

"You classify us by castes, and sentence us to life-long condemnation if we happen to be born in the wrong one, you Brahman pig," I heard Parvati spit. I had never seen her so upset.

Professor Kumar continued his lecture, stressing, "One cannot be a Hindu unless you recognize the sanctity of the Vedas. The constitution of India implies that being Hindu requires recognizing the Vedas."

He started to sound like a broken record. I understood the books were important. Why did he keep stressing it?

Suddenly Parvati jumped up and screamed, "How can you defend books written by men, men like you, probably stoned like pigs, God knows how many years ago, that condemn us to castes like cattle?"

Professor Kumar smiled and stated with authority, "That is such a tired argument. What other society does not have distinctive social classes? Europe struggled over the last decennia with the realization that classes are a structural reality in society. Half the time, people study utopian ideals in which classes would vanish. I do not pronounce judgment, but those ideals will fail. Consider this: What other society puts its priests and scholars in a higher social class than its warriors? Does that not reflect a healthy priority?"

Professor Kumar was a clever man. He was well read, and he understood how left-wing ideologies in Europe were bankrupting themselves and increasingly being questioned by the European intelligentsia. A lot of us had not caught on to that yet. By playing to the pacifistic tendencies of the people listening to him that night, he seemed to make a very clever observation to us, his gullible public.

Parvati was not to be silenced. "But the untouchables—the Dalits, the Sudras—are condemned to eternal suffering because of letters written on a piece of paper, interpreted by privileged men for their own interest.

Talk about that reality, too. Why don't you tell them how people in India avoid even walking in the shadows of the untouchables? How they are consigned to a life of poverty and misery because they are born Dalit, condemned by the Vedas to the trash heap of society?"

Professor Kumar replied calmly, matter-of-factly, but in a very condescending tone. "My sweet girl, hearing your accent, I assume you were born and raised in India. I do not know how you ended up here, or why you attack the fundamental aspects of India's social fabric. Be more critical about the theories the West feeds you and respect your own culture. Tradition is not, by definition, bad. Maybe you are Jain, or Muslim, Christian, or Buddhist. You are not Hindu; otherwise, you would not speak this way. You disrespect the foundations of our society. Why do you not sit down now?"

Parvati did not sit down. Still standing, she shouted, "Why is it that every time we question our society, we are damned for not respecting our culture? What do we have to do to destroy the caste system? Every day, more of us escape the stranglehold of our country to travel abroad. We learn, we study, and we will return to India and shake the very foundations of the society. You can set your saffron soldiers on me, you pig, rape me or kill me. I am only a Sudra, you Brahman swine, hardly worth talking to, but I am a Hindu and can question your holy Vedas. You cannot deny me that."

Professor Kumar's facial expression changed after this rebuttal. He was upset and no longer spoke to the auditorium. His answer was directed at Parvati.

"We are here to stay; we were always here, and we will rule again. Hindustan will rise again. We are Hindu, and India will be Hindu. My culture—my religion—will prevail, and be forewarned; violence will come. A tide is building that you cannot stop. You never could stop us—not centuries ago, not now. We are chosen, blessed by our writings with intellectual superiority and an eternal moral compass. You must understand that we have to fulfill our destiny."

Parvati left abruptly for the entrance. She turned at the entrance and shouted, "You fed the world 'truths' for thousands of years and perverted countries and societies, fathers and mothers, sons and daughters. But you will never be able to deal with people who just say no to these truths, with those who read your Vedas and show them for what they are—a program to keep the status quo, where the winners stay winners and the losers, losers. You want them to believe they can change their destiny in the next life, to trust and be good. Tell them about Charvaka. Why do you not? Why do you not tell them that Mother India, this spiritual source of light, this country revered for her gurus and metaphysical explorations, was also the country that first said no to the existence of God, to belief in an afterlife? That would be dangerous for you. What to do with people who do not believe in heaven or hell, good or bad? What do you do with people who reject the wisdom of 'Holy Books' and condemn them for what they are—letters on a page written by men. What to do with people that believe in this world, live here, and want to enjoy the here and now, who want to consume the pleasures of life in all its extremes?"

"How do you know his name?" asked Professor Kumar, disturbed. "They should not hear his name. Nobody should hear his name. Get out; go home. You abrahmana, how dare you question me? We are the most spiritually enlightened beings because we have never allowed those ideas to take root. And look at our society; respect is a constant, and elders are revered. We are the biggest democracy in the world; we will one day be the most populated country in the world. We will be a superpower. And you question the way we organize our society. I would rather have you live in our system, be a part of it, and support it."

The atmosphere in the auditorium had grown very uncomfortable. We were witnessing a conflict originating in one of the oldest and most revered cultures in the world, and we did not understand. What I understood was that the exchange between Professor Kumar and Parvati was nasty and hateful. They were both upset beyond what would be reasonable in a normal conflict. They were shouting at each other, ignoring the rest of the people in the auditorium. What should have been an evening about a country of religious and social tolerance, regressed into a shouting match with vague references to a terrible and divisive struggle stretching back thousands of years.

That night, in one of the smallest countries in Europe, a discussion between two foreigners from a far away continent descended rapidly into a ludicrous exchange peppered heavily with hyperbole. That was not new for most of us. Topics were discussed with vigor in those days, and every night there was a discussion somewhere—heavy on ideology, light on relevance. Hardboiled tactics were sometimes used, and yes, fists sometimes flew when points had to be made; being a student at this university was being part of that. But we defended ideology in our debates; we never attacked a person for where he came from, his background, or religion. We had made those mistakes in Europe, and millions paid for it with their lives. The personal nature of the argument between Professor Kumar and Parvati was a throwback to darker times.

Little did I realize that they were the norm and we the exception in the world. Just look at the numbers. Europe is so insignificant.

Just before Parvati made her final exit, she shouted at the top of her voice, "Tonight we make a lingam. I will celebrate my religion, being Hindu, and our real culture, and thank Charvaka!"

"You Kali whore. Beware of the consequences!"

Until then, I had followed the discussion with a mixture of astonishment and disbelief. I did not understand what was going on. But when the little professor in his long robe and orange shawl (so it was to me, color-blind as I am) called Parvati a whore, I stormed down and took a swing at him. Other students stopped me before I could reach him and dragged me to the entrance, intending to throw me out.

One of the event's organizers stopped them, turned to me, and said, "He is a representative of a foreign culture and a respected teacher. He is an authority on his country, and you want to start a fight with him? What is the matter with you and your girlfriend?"

"He calls her a whore, and I cannot do anything about it because he represents a foreign culture? What is that nonsense?"

"You keep quiet and listen, or follow your girlfriend out. It is your choice. Freedom of speech is an absolute principle between these walls."

I calmed down, sat again, and listened.

Professor Kumar looked with contempt in my direction, but continued his lecture.

"I apologize for this outburst; you were confronted with an Indian problem of which most people are unaware. My country is going through many changes and they are not always accepted. But is that not what democracy is all about?"

He continued his lecture, "The Indian constitution was drafted in 1950. Doctor Ambedkar, a Dalit, or untouchable, who earned a law degree from Columbia University, chaired the drafting committee. I am sorry the angry little girl who just left could not hear that our constitution was guided by the poorest in the country.

"The Indian constitution has 395 articles and ten appendices. It is one of the longest and most detailed in the world. It is also one of the most frequently amended. We change our constitution regularly, as others change clothes for each season, but not all those changes have made it a better constitution, or one that expresses the real desires of society. Some people in the Indian intelligentsia feel that the constitution does not adequately reflect the Hindu culture."

After this statement, he stopped, looked at us for a moment, and then continued.

"I am one of these persons. I believe our constitution should be a reflection of the essence of Indian culture, possibly the oldest culture in the world, with a spiritual depth to be found nowhere else in history or on the planet. But before I tell you more about that, I need to take you on a short tour through our writings—the Hindu scriptures.

"The earliest Hindu writings are the Vedas. They are written in a language with unprecedented lyrical subtleties. The Vedas are long and very complex. It takes more than one lifetime to master them. They are five to six times the length of your Bible. Maybe now you understand why we believe in reincarnation—we have to come back a number of times, just to understand our own Bible."

He looked with a sly, slight smile at the auditorium, to see if his attempt at humor had any effect. I do not remember if it did.

Professor Kumar went on for thirty minutes about the Hindu scriptures. Exotic terms that we had all heard at one time or another were put into context and chronological order. The Ramayana, the Mahabharata, the Bhagavad Gita, the Kama Sutra, they all passed in review. I am convinced that after the lecture, the bookshop did a brisk business selling these works.

It was only when he started to touch on the Sutras that he caught my attention again. His clear sympathy for the Sutras fired my interest. The Indian rulebooks, or law books, describe the tasks of the various castes that run like veins through Indian society. Castes are an intrinsic part of the history and society of India. This classification is probably the single most important feature Westerners describe when talking about India, beside the Taj Mahal, of course. The caste system is, for most of us, an obnoxious idea, impossible to square with the democratic ideals we are brought up with.

That night, Professor Kumar questioned those ideals, using the caste system as a metaphor to analyze Western society. He did not wait for his young public to attack the caste system. He reflected on existing inequalities in our society to make his points.

"Here in Belgium, a wide variety of hierarchical divisions exist. You have the haves and the have-nots. Some of you are here because the Belgian state finances your education; others are here funded by their family's money. Are Dutch-speaking citizens treated the same as the French-speaking? You have superior people and inferior people. My Aryan forefathers had the wisdom and insight to realize that these divisions are a constant of society. They formalized it in an economic and fair way. The Rig Veda, the very first Veda, mentions these divisions, again showing foresight and deep knowledge, a fountain of eternal bliss.

"People tend to classify themselves into castes or groups. We have workers and servants. They go to work under somebody else—that happens all over the world—that's the *Sudra* caste. We have merchants and farmers, who are self-motivated. They are the production units of the world, the providers. That's the *Vaishya* caste. We have politicians and lawmakers, law-enforcement, and the military. That's the *Kshatriya* caste. And then you have the priests, ministers, philosophers, and scholars. That's the *Brahman* caste. Every society has these four castes working within it, in one way or another. I belong to the Brahman caste. And as I said before, it is a credit to the wisdom of my forefathers to have placed the priests and philosophers at the top of society.

"You may now understand what the poor girl was screaming about before, about being a Sudra. For the Marxist-Leninists here tonight, human nature cannot be changed. One cannot invent a new man. Marx's knowledge pales in comparison to millennia-old insights. You can pass a law to abolish the caste system, but the law is helpless in a confrontation with nature and man's desire for differentiation. What is the use of laws, when we know society is based on color, gender, money, and education—on inequality! Human beings, on an almost genetic level, organize themselves with a strong yearning for these inequalities, and India is one of the largest working units in the world. The strength of this idea lies in our numbers."

I do not know if Professor Kumar convinced anybody that night. He possessed a certain erudition. His analyses appealed to common sense and were very persuasive. None of us had the insight to confront him with the hierarchical implications of the castes and the imprisonment of generations of people in them. None of us realized that his view of the caste system was just that— the view of one person. We did not confront him, because most of us did not know enough about it. Maybe we should have listened more closely.

"As a Hindu, I believe very strongly that stressing the supposed undemocratic nature of the caste system is a practice of other religions and politically unsavory forces to show us in a bad light. All countries have castes and divisions. Our caste system is simply a smart division of labor—a way to organize—and you will not remove this from society.

"I read recently in the Bombay Times, 'Those who convert from Hinduism to Christianity, Buddhism, and Islam still face separation on the basis of caste. There are separate churches in South India for Brahman converts and Sudra converts.'

"When I say I want a more Indianised constitution, I simply state that I want to see a return to some of our original law books. I do not want a constitution that reflects the Western views of our colonizers. I want a return to the Manu Smriti, a law book written by Manu, a pandit, a sage, a man well versed in Sanskrit, who projected the pure intentions of the Veda."

Professor Kumar, whose body language had changed throughout the lecture, spit out the last words. He stood erect now, striking a pose, staring us in the eyes.

"Any questions?"

He did not intend to answer any. He continued his lecture with increasing vigor and zeal.

"The Vedas are the ultimate source of knowledge. The Vedas say, 'Truth is one; the wise call it by different names.' You can be Christian, Muslim, or Jew; if you are searching for the truth, you follow a Hindu maxim. We contain you."

Professor Kumar looked around the room and said, "Your search for truth, on a meta-level, was always written in the Vedas. The Gospel of John, chapter 1, verse 1, says, 'In the beginning was the word, and the word was with God, and the word was God.' Centuries before, the Vedas mention the same idea. Read the Vedas, and you will come across concepts and ideas repeated in the quantum theories of Niels Bohr. I know of quantum physicists who use metaphors from Hindu religion to explain the most advanced ideas of humankind. When Robert Oppenheimer saw the first atom bomb explode, he referred to the Vedas-inspired Bhagavad Gita. 'I am death, devourer of all.'

"The Vedas are a reflection of the eternal laws of nature. The Vedic writings contain the principles of physics, mathematics, medicine, and astronomy. Modern science and the Vedas are just different names for the same eternal maxims. The texts are there for all to read, and if you do, you will conclude as I do—the Vedic-Aryan civilization was the origin of world civilization."

It was quite a statement to make in the center of one of the staunchest Catholic countries in the world, at a Catholic university with a philosophic tradition that could be traced back centuries—a university that considered Judeo-Christian thinking the cradle of civilization and morality. But the latest wave of philosophical fashion, bearing a distinctive French flavor, would have us believe that the Western model of reality was an autocratic and imperialistic way of acquiring knowledge. Modern Western science—defined in the past as an objective way to acquire knowledge—was now just another culturally dependent way to look at reality. The pinnacle of our Judeo-Christian enlightened worldview, it was unmasked as just another way of colonizing the world. With this wisdom, we seemed to lose every critical faculty.

Years later, I realized that however strong the arguments were for the thesis of Western scientific imperialism, we forgot to see the imperialism in this new wave of philosophy, with its strong tendency to explain everything in one word, one concept—

33

deconstruction, desire, Other, and so on. It was just another attempt to find a unified field theory in the world of ideas.

All is relative, but we forgot the relativity of relativism. In our day-to-day dealings with evil and problems, knowing that all is relative gives little guidance or relief. Knowing all is relative does not stop me from having to make daily decisions. It does not give me reprieve from having to see, feel, and hear evil. It does not stop me from being confronted with the shortcomings of others, or my own. I have to interact with others, imperfect others; there is no escaping that. Everybody needs to make decisions all the time.

Is it not more a question of scaling? Look at a woman from a distance, and she looks perfect. See her up close, and you see her imperfections. Become intimate, and she will be a goddess. What looks like a good deed or policy today is a disaster and a selfish act later. Chaos looks like perfect order if you view it from far enough away, and order can become total chaos, coming closer. This approach works not only for distance, but also for time. Everything can be everything, depending on distance in time and space—ten years or a thousand—my village, or the world. So any decision can be everything. Use the right scale, and it makes sense; use the wrong one, and it looks like chaos.

Is everything relative? Of course, but only when you change the scale. Most of the time, we do not have that luxury. Most of the time, we have to stay within one scale. This is just another guide for survival, to be adapted as time goes on, but this outlook works for me now.

That night, at Professor Kumar's lecture, I was confronted with old Eastern knowledge. It would take time before I realized that the label of Eastern knowledge was arbitrary, before I realized that this Vedic knowledge, presented as the pinnacle of Eastern knowledge and sensibilities, actually had Western flavors, too. Having been developed for millennia in the East, the Vedas would bite us in the ass as divine inspiration for some of the most horrific political systems ever created. We would create a superior Aryan being out of the knowledge and experiences of a dark-skinned continent and its deep-rooted Eastern philosophy. Who made whom? It was a question of scaling in time and distance. It depends on how you measure time, on the geographical scale you use. Go far enough back, and cause and effect change place. Look beyond your own country and culture and see its dependence on other countries and cultures. Is there ever a first cause?

Sometimes people are caught up in these movements, these accidents in history, and when they take a stand, they die. Sometimes people are too rigid to see they are using a scale reflecting time and geographical distance; they become dangerous.

At the end of Professor Kumar's lecture, I walked out of the auditorium. Parvati was waiting for me outside. We walked in silence toward her apartment.

Chapter 4

Catholic University of Leuven:
A Murder, a Lingam, a Rite

Belgium, 1981

"*C*ome inside," the policeman said.

He invited me with a flick of his hand to sit at a little metallic table with a green top. The chair was also metal and hurt my back. I remember thinking it had to be standard in any interrogation situation, but when I saw that the policeman was sitting on the same kind of chair, I attributed it to a lack of attention to ergonomics.

"Your name?"

"Jan Moore."

"That doesn't sound Belgian."

"It isn't. I think a great or great-great-grandfather came from England."

The policeman continued asking me all the standard identification questions. When he finished filling in the form in front of him, he leaned back and asked, "Tell me what you did last night from seven o'clock onwards?"

"Why?"

"Because I want to know!"

"Why? This morning when I got up, a van full of policemen was waiting; they grabbed me as I left my house and brought me here. Why? What did I do? Can I call a lawyer? Do I need a lawyer?"

The policeman threw a photo on the table. I saw a mangled body on a carpet, naked, with blood all around it. I saw signs in a strange language covering the walls. My stomach turned, and my breathing became erratic. I recognized the face. It was Parvati, obviously dead, sprawled on a carpet in her apartment.

Bhairava is the most terrifying avatar of Shiva. Frowns, large animal teeth, nakedness, and a string of skulls all contribute to the horror of his appearance. Black dogs were often sacrificed in his honor, as he is often portrayed with a black dog at his side. The dog licks the blood dripping from a human head in Shiva's hand.

"She died in a perverse ceremony, or rite, or whatever the hell it was. She died performing a ritual for the Indian god Shiva. That is all we know. I have some people going to the Oriental Studies department at the university to get further clarification. I do know that she was not supposed to die in this ritual, but she did; she was murdered. Her head was smashed in with a stone. You were seen leaving with her around ten last night from an auditorium in the philosophy department, and several witnesses stated she looked very upset."

I tried to breathe normally. Tears came into my eyes. I had lost my girlfriend. I realized, staring at the picture, that there was a lot I did not know about her. I was angry; she looked like she had been raped, beaten. I wanted to hit somebody. I cracked, started crying, and slammed my fists on the table. The policeman left the room, and I stayed behind, alone. I did not understand how Parvati had been found in these circumstances. I had left her after midnight, and she was ready to go to bed. Sure, she was upset about the lecture, but how could she have ended up like this? Then I remembered. What had she shouted just before she left the auditorium? *Tonight we make a lingam.*

I had forgotten about it, until now. There was so much that I never knew about her. I would never know. What was a lingam? Was it why she was dead?

The Kapalikas, or skull-bearers, who usually live on cremation grounds or in the forest, dedicate their lives to Bhairava. They are renowned for their magical powers, sexual hedonism, cannibalism, and liberal use of intoxicating substances. They are believed to command storms and floods. Smeared in ashes from cremations, they strike fear into others. They scoff at austerity and conventions. A well-known writing, the Kulanarva Tantra, offers this: "The adept should drink and drink again until he falls on the ground. If he gets up and drinks again, he will be freed of rebirth. Lord Bhairava de-

39

lights in their swooning, and their vomiting pleases all the gods."

The policeman returned with some coffee. He said, "Look, we're pretty sure you didn't do this. If you want to call a lawyer, you can. I don't want you having a lot of trouble. Just tell me a bit more about yourself and the girl in the picture, and I will see what I can do to get you out of here."

I told him Parvati was my girlfriend. I told him I really loved her and that we'd gone to a lecture on Indian religion the night before. I told him Parvati stormed out of the lecture, irritated. I explained that I found her outside the auditorium and that we left together. I told him I thought she was upset about something I asked, but that she later explained that she was angry with Professor Kumar and the things he said. I explained that I did not fully understand why she was angry, but that it must have had something to do with a caste conflict. I told him I left her home at midnight, and that I thought she asked me to leave because she was distressed and did not want me to see her like that. The policeman did not appear to be listening.

"She's dead," the policeman said. "I want to know who did it and why. We're a Catholic country, for God's sake. We have sex behind closed curtains and in total privacy. We do not play strange games. Now we have to see a girl raped or killed, or both, with a stone?" The policeman realized then that I was another victim of this tragedy.

"Look," he said. "I know you didn't do it. A witness saw six or seven people enter her home around midnight. He said they were all foreigners—Indian or Pakistani—dark-skinned."

I left the police station in shock. This morning, I woke up an average student with an exotic girlfriend. A few hours later, I had a dead girlfriend, and I had lost direction. I locked myself in my room and did not leave for a week. The friends I lived with brought me food and newspapers every day. I called home a lot. My parents visited, but everything was a blur. I remember my father more upset than understanding, because his son's name was linked to one of the most gruesome murders ever committed in Belgium. There was a huge hole in my chest that I could not fill.

For the entire week, my name was in every paper, and every social theorist wanting to garner attention opined about what had happened. Multi-culturalism was questioned and everything was placed in the wider context of a world run amok, youths having no frame of reference—all the heroes were dead. The fact that unemployment was high was apparently a moot point. The football hooligans did not help, either. What about gothic music and the occult? Reasons for Parvati's death were everywhere.

Then the Japanese cannibal Issei Sagawa killed and ate a Dutch student, and Parvati's murder was pulled from the front page. The cycle of rationalizing odd events began again. I was alone in my room, with my pain, missing Parvati.

When Brahma the creator created Kama, or the desire to confuse and seduce people, he handed arrows to Kama, who, an Indian version of Cupid, tested the arrows immediately on Brahma himself. As a result Brahma lusted after his own daughter. Shiva could not accept this. In a wrath of anger, he cut one of Brahma's five heads off. The head stuck to his hand, and although Shiva was a god, penitence had to be made. He took a vow to wander the world as a beggar until the head fell from his hand. On his wanderings, Shiva appeared as Bhairava to some holy men practicing austerity. They were suddenly confronted with a naked, sensual, dancing personification of Shiva. Their wives could not resist him and fell for his seductive powers. He performed erotic acts with them, sometimes in front of their husbands, who cursed his phallus.

I thought all the time about the night we went to the lecture and what happened there. Professor Kumar and Parvati showed real physical hate for each other that night. Maybe Professor Kumar had something to do with her death. When I explained my suspicions to the police later, they said that Professor Kumar had a water-tight alibi. His wife vowed he was home long before midnight and had not left the house until the next morning, after Parvati's body was found. He was no longer a suspect.

In the Shiva Purana, an ancient history on Shiva, it says that the world will not find peace until a receptacle is found for Shiva's sexual organ. In order to calm his phallus, he wants a pedestal in the form of a vagina. Some devotees want to stress that Bhairava devotion requires a liberal attitude towards sexuality, a lot of drinking, and more than the occasional screw. I feared that what happened in Belgium—the death of the Indian girl—was a deviant reverence to Bhairava with dark origins and a terrible misunderstanding of what Bhairava devotion should be.

The beheading of Brahma is the key. He is a symbol for the Brahmans. The Vedic laws prescribe that he who kills a Brahman shall live life as a solitary wanderer in the forests, living on handouts, confessing his crime, and using the skull of the Brahman as a bowl. That is the Bhairava myth, but you will always find people who see in the holy texts a means to their own end.

I recognized the photo at the top of the printed article. "Deviant phallus cult to blame, says Professor Kumar." A long interview with Dr. Kumar appeared in *Humo*, a leftist-leaning, semi-alternative magazine in Belgium. The magazine, mainly known for its cartoonists, published a long article on Parvati's murder. It had been two weeks since her death, and no arrest had been made; Parvati became an unsolved dossier in the annals of the Belgian justice system. She was, after all, just a visiting student from a far away place. The article continued.

Certain deviant rites are practiced as devotion to Shiva. Some believe that a link to Shiva or Bhairava can be created through certain activities and behavior. These devotees believe they can take on the powers of Shiva—become one with him. They believe they will receive magical powers to seduce women, have a long life, and have luck in chance games.

When a rite to Bhairava or Shiva takes place, you first need a symbol for Shiva's penis—a lingam. The lingam needs to be of natural material: a stone or a bone. You need a male participant and a female one. They clean themselves with warm water. The female participant chants "Om nama sakti" continuously, with her legs spread as wide as possible. The male rubs sandalwood paste over the female's feet with his fingers, chanting also. The male draws, with the paste, eight circles around the female's vagina, three lines across her body, a square upon her throat, and a downward-pointing triangle upon her forehead. The male then makes sure the woman is lubricated through various techniques, such as the use of breath and seductive eye contact, making sure he never touches her body. Then the male takes the lingam, sometimes with honey poured over it, and places it into the vagina of the female, making sure it causes light bleeding. The lingam must be firmly in place and stay in place on its own. A leaf of grass is fastened tightly around the thighs of the female. Now further physical contact is allowed, and the female is brought to orgasm. Afterwards, the lingam is removed and bathed in warm water.

I stopped reading for a moment; Parvati was found in circumstances very much as Professor Kumar described. I had seen the paintings on her body, the grass leaves around her thighs, in the picture the policeman showed me. She made her lingam that night, after I left her. She was a Shiva devotee.

Devotees believe that worship of Shiva demands extreme acts of a sexual nature with very violent overtones. People go into orgiastic trances and lose control. In the West, it would probably be called a "crime of passion." A fringe group of poorly informed people, Kapalikas, performs the rituals. Every religion has fanatics and offshoots that adopt sexually deviant activities. Catholicism had a number of these orders in the Middle Ages. Taoism, Tibetan Buddhism—each had versions of sexually based religious practices. Masturbation has been widely used in Judeo-Christian circles to reach exhaustion and find a path to spiritual enlightenment. I consider this a deterioration of one's moral fiber. The search for spirituality should not devolve into a hunt for personal pleasure. It hurts that so many in the West equate Hinduism with an exotic strand called Tantra. Hinduism incorporates various traditions; Tantra is one of them. It is a meditation and monogamous rite, not an orgiastic feast with satanic overtones. This kind of deviation, where personal pleasure becomes a goal in itself, leads to accidents like the one with the girl.

The article rambled on for a while about the relativity of cultural values and the need to understand everything in context. Professor Kumar sounded rational and reasonable. There was no trace of Professor Kumar's conviction that the Hindu culture was the basis for ours, and it should be upheld as a norm for everybody. Suddenly, he was a cultural relativist, stressing the otherness of Indian culture. Why did the journalist not ask him if he had something to do with her death? More importantly, why was the name Charvaka not featured? His name was found on the walls. The policeman had called me a few days after the first interrogation and asked if the name "Charvaka" meant something to me. He had had all the strange signs smeared on the walls translated. They were Sanskrit insults to abrahmanas, atheists, and Charvaka. The language was foul, hateful, and written with Parvati's blood. I told the police how Parvati had shouted Charvaka's name the night Professor Kumar was giving his lecture, but that I did not know anything more about him. How did he figure in the story?

Professor Kumar held back his most vitriolic condemnation of the Shiva rite and the persons carrying them out for the end of the article. Years later, I would understand that Professor Kumar was a newly emerging intellectual from the Indian elite, but with geographically wider ramifications, as the murder of Parvati in Belgium proved. He was at the forefront of the intellectual battle for the soul of India. He was at the forefront of a battle to manage the spirit of man, his desires, and common sense. He wanted to curb man's disdain for control and authority. He wanted man to be more than a pleasure-driven, pleasure-seeking animal.

Do not misunderstand; I am not advocating that humankind would be a better off, happier, or more moral being without that management. Probably quite the opposite. I just want to expose the puppet masters.

Look at us Hindus. India is our ancestral land and the land of our religion. Misinformed historians think the Aryans invaded India, and that Hindus descend from them. That is preposterous. The Aryans were always here, we descend directly from them, and as such, we are the inheritors of the land since the beginning of time. India is our motherland, and always was. Hindus are indigenous, and the Muslims and Christians are not; their religions did not originate in India. But we are an inclusive religion. Anybody looking for truth can be called a Hindu, provided the sanctity of the Vedas is not questioned. Some fringe movements in Hinduism cling to the idea that there was a "before Hinduism." That is not possible. Even the earliest civilizations were Aryan at their roots. Our culture is not the result of barbarian invaders.

Misguided religious fanatics, looking for sexual gratification, make use of young girls to live out their fantasies, and kill them in the process. They are not real Hindus, it is not acceptable, and the culprits should be dealt with severely. These people think they are reliving

47

rituals that go back to the time of their forefathers, the Dravidians, a dark race of farmers. It is an imperialistic plot to divide India. Here in Belgium, this can be misunderstood, but people hanging on to these beliefs do our nation a great disservice, and perhaps they deserve their fate.

Professor Kumar stopped short of condoning the murder of Parvati. After reading the article and having seen him in the seminar, I was more convinced than ever that he had something to do with her death. I never confronted him. He returned to India soon after the murder.

I left Leuven a few months later. The perpetrators of the murder were never found. It took more than a decade before answers started emerging. I always knew I would end up working in India. It was stronger than I was. It was my destiny. I needed to find closure.

Chapter 5

Friday, March 12

Bombay, 1993

O n this day, Bombay was attacked with a barrage of bomb blasts that left more than 250 people dead and over a thousand wounded. The bombs were directed at the financial heart of the city, and India. The shockwave would expand for years to come. As usual, there was a lot of confusion over the identity of the perpetrators and their motivations. Numerous reports exist in which government officials pointed to the Tamil Tigers——fighting their version of a "historical right"—as the instigators of the blasts.

The Bharatiya Janata Party (BJP) quickly captured the scepter of judge and jury. They insisted Pakistan was behind the wave of destruction. The Muslim world, extremely upset with the destruction of the Babri Masjid mosque by the warriors of Ram some months before, had taken revenge forcefully. However, the destruction of the mosque, and the response to it, was no more than a blip in the long cycle of violence between Muslims and Hindus in India.

Today, the consensus is that the Indian version of a mafia don, Dawood Ibrahim, who controlled the Bombay underworld, was responsible. Supposedly, the Pakistani intelligence service recruited him and his associates to orchestrate the symphony of atrocities in March 1993. The ISI, the Pakistani intelligence services, had leverage on Dawood. He used the Pakistani-controlled shipping routes between Dubai and other Gulf nations and the Indian West Coast to make millions of dollars. They could take away his lucrative trade if they wanted. Dawood transported weapons and explosives the same way he transported his cigarettes, drugs, and Coca-Cola. In those days, any can of Coca-Cola Light arrived in India from Dawood's trade routes bearing Arabic letters.

Financing the bombing operation was easy using the hawala channels between the Gulf States and India. These channels were used to pay contract killers, informers, police, and anybody who needed to be bribed. It was a well-known secret of expatriates who worked in India in those days that Khar had a little hotel where you could bring your bags of rupees, however you earned them, and for a fee, hard currency would appear in an account in Dubai. Easy, clean, non-traceable. What choice was there, after all? The rupee could not be converted. It was much easier than trying to smuggle the rupees over the Indian border via a flight from Madras to Singapore, then changing the currency in the streets of Singapore. This was especially true since reports were starting to appear in the Indian newspapers mentioning foreigners caught at the border for currency smuggling and given jail sentences. In light of this, the fee for risk-free currency exchange was a minor inconvenience.

I will always remember Friday, March 12, 1993. It was only a few days after the Jain holy man had passed through Khar with thousands of people cheering and admiring his lifelong conviction to austerity and nonviolence.

Sony had answered many of my questions after I saw the Jain guru. He told me that some Jains take their vow of austerity so far that they effectively starve themselves and die. He told me Jain monks and nuns wear a piece of cloth over their mouths to prevent the accidental inhalation of an insect. He told me they brush the ground before they put down their feet to prevent squashing any life. He told me Jains could lead normal lives and be very successful. He told me about the schism that grew in the Jain religion between the devotees that walked around naked, and those who wore white clothing—a schism dating back hundreds of years. He told me that the most admired Jains are the ascetics who took the great vow or mahavrata. They are believed to have total self-control and can even influence their surroundings. Quite commonly, they spread a heat wave.

He told me of their doctrines of viewpoints and many-sidedness, a subtle philosophy that puts our Aristotelian-dominated logic to shame. And he told me how Jainism questioned the authority of the Vedas.

In the months after the blast, newspapers kept the stories going. The press had a field day when movie actor Sanjay Dutt, from the famous acting family of the same name, was arrested on charges of involvement in the bomb blasts. The fact that he had AK-56 rifles in his house (other sources say they were AK-47s), was Bollywood's bad boy, and had dabbled in drugs did not help matters, nor did the frequent reports of him hitting journalists.

The girls that I worked with in the office hung life-sized posters of the actor on the walls. He had given them hours of pleasure in the movie theaters of Bombay. Bollywood was alive and well before Hollywood discovered it. Dutt was probably the only actor in those days that Westerners would not have considered an overweight, middle-aged man doing bad dance routines. He had an impressive physique and bulging muscles. When he landed in jail, he lost his muscle mass and popularity.

Some months later, during a trip to Goa, I met an American man named Jay in the city of Panjim. My encounter with him brought back the memory of Parvati and gave it context. He clarified my position as a reluctant pawn in a millennia-old chess match.

We are all reluctant pawns in the theatre of life. I just had the luck to encounter the right people to give me insights into the forces driving my life. Not that these insights would give me any control—an illusion of control, maybe. An illusion of control is all we can achieve. But then again, that is all we need to survive.

Jay had been based in Goa for two years. He told me about the cheap drugs one could get on the beaches of Colva and Vagator, drugs he frequently tried. Old hippies, who all swore they had met the Beatles on their quest for spiritual truth, and young house and techno freaks mingled with each other, comparing mushroom teas to ecstasy. Every year, it culminated in a wild drug party in Vagator on New Year's Eve, probably the best beach party in the world.

Jay was a Mormon scholar from Brigham Young University. He was conducting an anthropological study in Goa for his doctorate. We had long discussions about India and the culture shock it presented to Westerners. We agreed on the not-so-original insight that religion permeates everything in India.

One day, during one of our hour-long conversations, he asked, "You ever heard of a fellow called Charvaka?"

I did not react to the question. I had not heard the name in more than a decade. It was connected to all I had tried to forget; it triggered memories of murder and the only girl I really loved.

"He was an atheist, the first in man's history. He believed in enjoying life. None of his writings survive. His followers were systematically massacred and silenced over the last millennia, but I heard they are still here in India. I heard that the bomb attacks in Bombay last March were actually directed at Charvaka's followers. Jains tried to kill some of Charvaka's followers. Can you make sense of that? Believers in nonviolence, killing other human beings? I will never understand this country."

"But I thought Pakistan and the Bombay mafia were responsible? Surely atheists are no reason to blow up half the town."

"That's what they want you to believe."

"Sorry, Jay, but who is 'they'?"

"The Brahmans. They have always controlled the world. They are master controllers; they invented control by religion. Even Joseph Smith could learn a thing or two from them. There were twelve or thirteen blasts in Bombay on March 12, but one victim was extra tragic. When they investigated the bomb that went off at the Searock Hotel in Bombay, they found in the ruins, beside many other dead bodies, the body of a naked woman with her head smashed in by a rock. It was kept out of the newspapers because it did not uphold the belief of Pakistan as the guilty party."

"A lingam," I whispered.

Jay looked at me in amazement. "Why do you say that? How do you know? But you're right; Shiva's penis had penetrated the girl's head."

I felt sick. How could this crime resemble a tragedy that happened ten years ago on the other side of the world, when I was a student? Again, the name of Charvaka was mentioned in connection to this crime. What was his relation to these murders?

Jay leaned over to me.

"What I am going to tell you is not to be repeated. I heard it from some elders before I arrived here. They met this traveling guru, or whatever you call them, who talked to them about the Brahman conspiracy."

Where had I heard this before? Like an old dream coming back, a déjà vu that festered like acid in my brain, I remembered. Parvati had told me about this.

"When the English traders were confronted with Indian society in the 1600s, they encountered a society without a consistent body of law. There were only writings, called Sutras—rules and moral codes dealing with day-to-day life, household practices, sacrifices, customs relating to marriage, death, and so on."

"I've heard of them," I said.

"Indian society was a body of self-governing communities, guided by the Sutras and local sages. Each community developed its own customs to deal with life and its conflicts. There was no consistent justice, nor any attempt to create a uniform body of law.

"The English found it frustrating; it went against their sense of 'fair play' to deal with radically opposing punishments in different crimes. Each community could introduce new customs or change existing ones any time they wished."

"Governance by the people, for the people," I thought aloud.

Jay nodded and continued, "To rectify the situation, the English, with the help of local pandits, learned men, tried to create a set of uniform Hindu laws that would govern all conflict resolution. There were some problems. The term 'Hindu' was problematic. People defined their identity through caste, language, region, and the sects to which they belonged. Ask a person on the street here in Goa what his nationality is, and they will proudly answer Goan. The same in Kerela, and all over India. The Goans are proud of their Portuguese heritage. For God's sake, they still wear their mustaches and beards the way Portuguese men did decades ago. You want to look up a land title here, anything older than 1962 needs to be translated from Portuguese. My point is that there is no Hindu nation or national identity. Even the Vedas never mention Hindu or Hindustan.

"Quite arbitrarily, the English chose the 'Manu Smriti,' written by the pandit Manu, as the basis of a Hindu jurisprudence. But was it really arbitrary? The English ran India with help of the Indian elite. The Brahman elite ran the courts and made sure the English chose Manu's writings as the basis for a unified law. The English believed fair play was restored and that they were running India according to universal Hindu principles. The English, brilliantly manipulated by the Brahman caste, chose a book that favored Brahmans over all other castes and used it as the basis for a fair and universal law.

"Then the Brahman elites went further. They encouraged the Indian people to look for independence from their colonial masters. The same Brahman elites that cooperated with the English in establishing jurisprudence in favor of their caste sought independence now. They were always in the background in the independence struggle, lurking, ready to revive a Brahman-ruled Aryan nation. They were smart; they used the concept of 'India as One Nation' as a rallying point in the independence struggle. They convinced the nation of the glory of 'ancient India,' or Hindustan and the importance of Sanskrit, although less than one percent of the population spoke that language. That India had never been a united country and Hindustan had never referred to India as a whole, but to only a part in the north, was kept hidden. Revisionism is rampant in every culture, and India is no exception.

"But something worse happened; the masses received an Aryan brainwashing. The Brahmans brought their Vedas and the Manu Smriti into the foreground to govern India. Now the story becomes interesting. Since the conception of the Indian constitution, the Brahmans have tried to discredit it. Just after independence, they had to be careful. They had mobilized the masses to throw the English out and could not risk antagonizing those masses themselves, but they did not like the Indian constitution because a member of the lowest caste, an atheist Buddhist, wrote it. Doctor Ambedkar was not one of them. That a lower caste member was responsible for the creation of the constitution made for great public relations, but for the Brahmans, the constitution lacked compliance with the Indian ethos; it missed the Vedic flavor and should not be obeyed by true believers."

I had heard some of the things Jay was telling me a long time ago, in the lecture on Hindu religions by Professor Kumar. Jay, however, came from the opposite side. Where Professor Kumar had been a proponent and defender of the Brahman cause and caste system, Jay seemed exceptionally critical of them, as Parvati had been. I could not understand how, more than ten years after I first heard of the Brahman caste, Jay was opposing the ideas Professor Kumar had propounded. It was not mainstream thought, so finding a stranger in a country thousands of miles away from my homeland talking about the Brahman influence on society and history was more than a bit odd. Was it a coincidence, or was I missing something?

Jay continued, "It becomes really interesting when one starts looking at the precepts one finds in the Manu Smriti—untouchables, Dalits, and Sudras live outside the village and can only own dogs and donkeys, reflecting the Brahman-Aryan view that untouchables are merely animals themselves.

"When an untouchable, Dalit or Sudra, insults a higher caste, his tongue should be cut out, according to Manu. Manu and the Vedic Aryans considered lower castes to be dark-skinned animals. Note how similar this sounds to some of the arguments used by white supremacist bigots. I am sure you can find groups of people that think the same in Europe, even today. According to Manu, it is acceptable for a Brahman to take the possessions of his Sudra slaves, for they cannot have property. When you see the scams in India, you have to think the rule is still obeyed to perfection; it may help explain the enormous differences in wealth distribution.

"It's worse for women. They cannot own property. They are to be devoured by dogs if they question their lord and master, the man to whom they belong. There are some hair-raising prescriptions in Manu's book. It is the Brahmans' goal to incorporate the prescriptions of Manu Smriti into the Indian constitution and erode its democracy. The Brahmans want to further Aryan domination. India has been a battlefield of Brahman supremacists and those who oppose the Brahmans for millennia. The opposition is the abrahmanas or non-believers, and the non-Aryan descendants of the original Sudra population that lived in India before the Aryans conquered it: the Dravidians. You're probably wondering what all of this has to do with the murder in Bombay today."

I nodded.

"The program the Brahmans were running was and is strongly opposed. The Jains and the Buddhists began as opposition movements against the Brahmans. Going back to around 600 BC, the Brahmans, the Aryan priests, had a quasi-unchallenged position in Indian society. They were masters of secret rituals. They convinced the population that the rituals were necessary to keep balance in the world. The rituals became goals in themselves. The gods for which these rituals were performed became less relevant than the rituals themselves.

"The Brahmans made money from this, which didn't help their case. People started reacting. This reaction was crystallized in so-called 'shramans'—seekers, wanderers, and ascetics—who reacted against the Brahmans they believed were misleading the masses. The shramans believed that the way to attain union with God was not by repeating empty rituals. We saw similar reactions in Protestant movements against the Catholic clergy in Europe.

"The Buddhist and the Jain movement were at the forefront of the rejection of Brahman ritual. Less known is that this was also a time when pretty extreme thinkers arrived, pure materialists who declared life after death was humbug, and sages that believed that the concept of sin was bogus.

"I once heard a story about an atomist who believed that hacking off somebody's head was not really murder because it was just slicing through eternal atoms, rearranging timeless atoms to suit one's needs. Many of these extreme thinkers orbited Charvaka. He was so dangerous that almost none of his writings or ideas survived. Together with the Jains and Buddhists, he turned against a ritualistic Brahmanism."

Charvaka? Always that name.

What had the policeman said? "We had the writings on the wall analyzed; they were written in a language called Sanskrit; a professor at the Oriental Institute translated them. They were mainly insults…"

Charvaka—pronouncing his name makes you a whore, and dead is your destiny. All non-believers need to be eradicated from the motherland; our day is here. Repent or die. Charvaka, son of a dog….

The words swam through my head. I could not remember the rest. All that was relevant for me was that Parvati died with his name in her blood on the wall.

Jay continued, "I don't know anything about him. Nobody really talks about him. His writings are gone. Maybe that fact alone makes him important. As I said before, I heard that the followers of a Jain guru tried to kill attendees in a sexual ritual that evoked or celebrated the ideas of Charvaka. It is as unnatural for a Jain to kill as water running up a mountain, but it was confirmed several times. I heard that an important Brahman instructed them to do the deed, and the Jains could justify it, as their religion allows them to protect themselves. They can kill if threatened, but I do not know if they were threatened, and if threatened, by whom or what? At the same time, the Brahmans used their power to organize another dozen bomb attacks in Bombay to cover up the one bomb that had an intentional target—Charvaka and his followers."

"But," I said, interrupting him, "that doesn't make sense! You just told me that the Jains, Buddhists, and Charvaka were part of an original opposition movement against the Brahmans. Why would they turn against each other?"

"Yes, but the Jains and Buddhists, unlike Charvaka, carried the seeds of Hinduism in their writings. Charvaka rejected everything in the Vedas outright. More importantly, the popularity of the Brahmans was diminishing, and the authority of the Vedas, their holy wisdom, was under attack. What could have been better for them than to divide their opposition? They were smart enough to allow some dissent, and if they had to allow dissent, better it come from opposition that was controllable and still reflected Vedic influence.

"Look at the results. For a dogmatic, tyrannical idea to survive, you need to release the pressure of dissident ideas once in a while. The Brahmans are masters at this. Look at India today—Buddhism has virtually disappeared, and the Jains are considered a fringe movement for people with masochistic needs. Brahmanism is alive and well under the name of Hinduism, and Charvaka is only a myth. None of his writings can be found. All we know of him comes from the writings of his opponents. Why the Jains and the Buddhists became so aggressively opposed to Charvaka, I do not understand. Why this feud continues is a mystery. You would think the Jains, Buddhists, and Charvaka's refusal to acknowledge the absolute authority of the Vedas or the Brahmans' elitist position would unite them, but the Jains and Buddhists united only in their common hatred for Charvaka, an opposition that seems a lot stronger than their opposition against their original foes, the Brahmans. Is this another ploy of the Brahmans? I don't know."

"Are you suggesting that the Jain and Buddhist movements made a pact with the devil against Charvaka for their own survival? A pact that survives to today?"

"You said it."

"But can ideas be that powerful? What was it that Charvaka and his followers were teaching that had to be erased? And why are people still murdered today over it?"

"There are almost no references left—none that I know of. But that people die for ideas is not new or limited to these cases. Europe probably killed more in the name of ideology than any other continent. Need I remind you of Christianity, communism, fascism?"

I bowed my head; Europeans were hardly in a position to criticize anyone. Ideologies, and belief in them, are bigger killers than any viruses our human bodies encounter. Perhaps we should investigate whether ideology, in some weird way, transforms into a virus that infects and turns us into sociopaths.

Just an idea!

Chapter 6

Catholic University of Leuven:
Parvati, a Sudra

Belgium, 1981

*H*er first words were a shouted question. "Do you know what you heard tonight?"

We were back in her flat after walking from the auditorium where Professor Kumar had given his lecture. "You heard the origin of all evil, an avatar of Hitler, a personification of Manu, the KKK's cry for supremacy, all wrapped up in an intellectual jacket that hides the festering body from which it emanates. Their program is as old as the human race; it is the great white Aryan conspiracy—more dangerous than ever, more hidden than ever, and more credible than ever. I am the Jew in the story, the victim of color, the victim of bias solidified in the oldest and most revered writings on earth."

Parvati fell on her knees, crying hysterically, "Can we never escape them?"

I went to the kitchen and fetched her something to drink. I did not know what to think or say. I did not understand the source of her anger. When I returned from the kitchen, she had calmed down. She started to speak before I could sit.

"Go back a couple thousand years. Your ancestors roamed what is now Eastern Europe. They were a strong people with big herds of domesticated animals that gave them milk, butter, and meat. They kept warm with the leather and wool of their animals. They did not pretend to be smart, and they had not a lot of artistic depth, but they loved their language. Their bards composed wonderful poems that talked about their adventures and conquests. They loved the poems so much they often blinded their bards to make sure they would not wander too far. They did not want to lose the only record of their deeds. They had no writing. They were primitive, tall, and white.

"Force and violence came naturally to these people. They enjoyed their vigor and the fear they struck in others. It was addictive and a source of strength for them, strength needed in confrontations with other cultures, which without exception were usually superior and more developed. Confronted with that sophistication, they did what they did best and made them feel good—they burned and destroyed. Their hunger for land grew as their population did. They domesticated horses and learned to sail, and with their bards singing their praises, they conquered foreign lands and people.

"Around 1500 BC, they arrived at the Indus and were confronted with an evolved civilization crystallized in two cities: Harappa and Mohenjo-Daro—where my ancestors came from. They were a very advanced society. The cities contained thousands of people, supported by elaborate agriculture. They built their houses with bricks, and most homes had a separate bathroom. My ancestors were aware of the importance of personal hygiene. They were small, sensitive, dark-skinned people. They had a written language and traded extensively with the outside world.

"My ancestors were shocked by the blonde giants singing Vedic hymns, eating mostly red meat, claiming the title of Aryans, or nobles. Nobles? They were savage and unclean. They could not read or write." Parvati sounded bitter.

"For the Aryans, weak, dark people were nothing new. They had met them before, enslaved them, and killed them. And history repeated itself. The advanced culture of my ancestors all but disappeared, but every confrontation between cultures is a two-way exchange. My ancestors, the Dravidians, intrigued the Aryans. They were so different, with such a strange religion. It was a culture shock that ripples on the pond of history today: ask any Westerner who has spent time in India.

"The Aryans liked space. They devoured it and usurped it. They lived under the wide skies, under the sun; life was an adventure. Their gods had to supply them with food, drink, attractive women, and victory in battle. Their gods were their friends, making the world a wonderful place; they did not insult their gods by trying to be saved from the world or pursuing esoteric truths. They had no thought of reincarnation. If the Aryans killed a man, they expected him to stay dead. Preferably, with no blood left in him. They did not want to kill the same enemy repeatedly."

Parvati had spoken the whole time with her head down. She looked up a moment, to make sure I was still paying attention, and continued her story.

"What a contrast with the dark-skinned people who lived around the Indus. They did not go forth under the bright sun in war parties. They were sedentary, hard-working farmers with a love for the earth and the moon, following their rhythms. The female earth and the masculine moon were a divine couple that provided for them. They did not look to the sun but to the moon to mark their seasons, to know the proper times to plant their seeds in Mother Earth.

"They knew the moon commanded ebb and flood and the fertility of their women. They knew their offspring took ten lunar cycles; they saw that semen was the color of the moon and menstrual blood was the color of the earth, especially when you looked at it under the moonlight. The moon was attracted to the earth as a man is to a woman, but the great distance between the moon and the earth was a cosmic tale of unfulfilled love drowning in a sea of desire. My ancestors could give their story a happy end; they could cross the divide and inseminate Mother Earth as a cosmic stand-in for the moon. Their life, past and future, was dependent upon the union between the earth and the moon." Parvati stopped.

I was silent. The sexual innuendos partly excited me, partly shocked me. It transformed my impression of a culture I had always perceived as sexually stoic and impotent. This erotic tale had survived for thousands of years; it was very enticing.

"The farmers went all the way to secure the union between moon and earth. Their sexual attraction had to be fulfilled. Their love had to be consummated. So the farmers allowed their priest to select somebody, feed and cherish him, and as the planting season began, and it was necessary for the moon to impregnate the earth, they roasted the fellow alive. Each scream of pain showed how much they were willing to endure for Mother Earth's love. Sometimes the fellow was sliced up raw in an orgiastic feast led by the priests, and each farmer completed the coitus between earth and moon by burying a piece of his meat in Mother Earth. A good crop was assured."

I was appalled.

"Why do you look so horrified?" Parvati asked, upon seeing the look on my face.

"Burning a man alive, slicing him up—that's barbaric."

"So were your witch burnings in Europe. The gassing of Jews in the Second World War. No one has a patent on irrational cruelty. At least our intention was creation, growth, sensuality."

She continued her story. "The Aryans, who knew a thing or two about killing, were shocked by the rituals, a theatre of sexual intercourse on a planetary scale. They did not understand why Mother Earth was depicted as ugly. Their goddesses were beautiful—much nicer to pray to and better to look at.

"Mother Earth was the ugliest woman they had ever seen. Kali—oh, she was inky-black, black as plowed earth, black as moonlit blood, black as the skin of the little, flat-nosed people praying to her. She had a blood-thirsty face and a necklace made of snakes and human skulls. Out of her open mouth, a tongue dripped with blood. Everywhere the Aryans looked, in temples and homes, they found phalli erected to serve her. The farmers could not understand the Aryans' consternation. What was more natural than a phallus, a lingam, a plow to impregnate Mother Earth?

"It was too much for the Aryan warriors. These dark little people with their strange rituals that seemed to cause them to lose all sense and become a fornicating mob were mad, only good enough to be slaves and laborers. They existed to make the lives of Aryans better. That was all.

"But Kali was patient and waited. The Aryans lost their love of roaming and their lust for battle. They no

longer wanted to see their sons die in battle. They
learned how the earth could feed them. They started set-
tling into agricultural groups.

"One group of Aryans, their priests, was intrigued by
the power the local priests had over their people. It was
awesome. Power they understood. They were attracted
and appalled at the same time, but they recognized a
good show when they saw one. They understood the
power of a good ceremony and an occasional sacrifice.
Burning bodies, slicing them up, having whole villages
participate in a theatrical production where the public
was made the carriers of semen between moon and
earth—it was a well-written piece. They saw people lose
their critical faculties, become slaves of their emotions,
giving themselves over to the priests who were orches-
trating the rituals like a planetary fornication party, and
they understood that their own beautiful hymns were no
match for the orgiastic psychedelic screams for Kali.

"They started some impressive productions of their
own. In one, a stallion was kept from ejaculating semen
for a whole year. The stallion roamed free, and everywhere it set foot, the land became land of the king."

"I'm sure that horny devil ran around a lot," I interjected, but Parvati paid no attention to my remark.

"After a year, the Aryan priests strangled the horse
and the king's wife had intercourse with the dead stallion."

"That gives a new meaning to necrophilia, bestiality,
and asphyxia, all in one go," I said. Parvati looked disturbed by my comment, but refrained from remarks.

"The Aryan priests developed and adapted a plan to control their warriors, my ancestors, and the world—not with the sword or violence, but with ideas packaged in a religious veneer. They were so masterful that all over the world, we still struggle with their genius. Marxism, fascism, and capitalism are ideas developed by provincial minds, compared to the genius and scope of the Aryan legacy.

"Confronted with a Dravidian population that was superior in numbers and knowledge, but inferior to the warriors of their own people, they changed their religious-magical ceremonies according to what they learned from the ceremonies of the Dravidians. Sacrifices became a central theme—cattle, goats, horses, and sheep were slaughtered in ritual killings to enthrall and fixate the population. They made sure to elevate the position of the leader of the ceremony—the priest. They started to call themselves *Brahmans*.

"At first Aryans had no written records; they were too barbaric—it took a while before their oral traditions and ceremonies were written in the Vedas. These Vedas were not a reflection of the Aryan culture; they were more a reflection of the culture shaped by the Aryans as they imposed social and religious totalitarianism on the Dravidian population. Whole societies, tribes, languages, populations, religions, and gods were condemned to the dustbin of history or usurped by the Vedic wisdom of the Brahmans. They gave Kali a makeover, and Shiva received an erotic, attractive wife named Parvati with hundreds of pages of poetry attributed to her beauty."

"So that's where—"

"Yes, that is where my name originates. Gods were promoted and demoted, given wives—all in the interest of the Brahman master plan of control. The Brahmans' genius lay in the fact that they adapted and learned; at least, this time they did.

"In the process, they created a caste system that, once written in Sanskrit, has controlled the Indian population to this day, preserving the hegemony of the Aryans over the population, and within this the hegemony, the power of the priests, the Brahmans."

Parvati was speaking faster and growing angrier as her story went on. I asked if she wanted to stop for a moment, but there was no stopping her now.

"Their biggest coup was yet to come. It took a couple of centuries to develop the concept, but then the Brahmans tacked on the concept of karma as an *ad hoc* addition to their Vedic writings. Now they had a blank check to the minds and riches of the people.

Divided in castes, people were eager to reach a higher caste in their next life. The Brahmans made sure the people could obtain this without having to lead a pious life. Good karma was for sale—currency that bought a better life next time around.

"The first three castes were exclusively for the white-skinned Aryans; the fourth class was for the black indigenous population, the Dravidians. They became the

Sudras, or slaves—the unclean underbelly of society. Later, a fifth caste was created, the untouchables—the Dalits. I suspect this was done to appease the Sudras. It is somewhat unclear. But what better way to control and keep the masses happy than to create a lower animal to blame? Many leaders throughout history have learned that lesson. Some people defend the caste system by saying that in its infancy, it was not a rigid system, just a practical way of organizing society. They defend it by saying in the early days, castes were not closed or exclusive, and movement between them was possible. They forget to mention that even in those days, movement was only possible for the Aryans; my ancestors were enslaved in the fourth caste.

"For more than a thousand years, the system worked like a dream—for the ruling classes. The white-skinned invaders led happy, easy lives. The Vedas were the basis of religion, not to be questioned, and the religious writings supported the caste system as desired by the gods. How could you question the will of the gods? How do you question the Bible or the Koran? The Vedas were written in a language that few mastered, but that surely contributed to their mystic qualities—secret utterances that only a chosen few, the Brahman priests, could formulate, and with that formulation, condemn you to riches or poverty, heaven or hell.

"Do you understand what happened?" Parvati asked me. "Do you understand that in a couple of decennia, India was conquered by a handful of inferior people and a few priests with a religious dynamic second to none in the history of the world? They created a body of beliefs that put them at the top of a hierarchical system that allowed them to become the most dangerous puppet-masters in the world. Every time they encountered competing religions, they absorbed them, incorporated them. Look at Hinduism today. The glorious religions of my ancestors—Shaivists, followers of Shiva; Shaktists, followers of Shakti, the consort of Shiva; and Tantrism—have disappeared into a religious black hole created by the Brahmans, their followers degraded and made slaves."

I nodded, but felt a bit skeptical about the dramatics of her story. Conspiracies on a global scale were the stuff of Bond movies. I was no specialist, but Tantrism, Shiva—surely, these were integral parts of the Hindu religion. I kept these thoughts to myself, though.

"Do you know why Professor Kumar was so rude to me? He saw me as a lesser being, an outcast. I was not supposed to question him. I am a reminder of a pre-Brahman, pre-Veda era, a religious rebel who will not recognize his stupid Vedas. I am a reminder of those slaughtered by the Aryans—the Dravidians. We live on as Sudras and Dalits."

I understood Parvati was deeply hurt. Nobody likes being called a whore in an auditorium full of people, but to conclude that the professor was the personification of evil was a bit much. Besides, I probably wanted to sleep with Parvati that night, and as upset as she was, I did not see that happening. I did not help matters by entering into a discussion with her.

"Parvati," I tried carefully, "are you saying that the Indian man in the auditorium tonight was the mouth-piece of a worldwide conspiracy to put descendents of the Aryans who invaded India, centuries ago, in command of the world?"

She looked up and asked, "Have you not listened to a word I've said?"

"Yes, but surely you're blowing it out of proportion!"

"Jan, you haven't known me that long yet; I want to take my time and explain, because I want you to understand. Maybe I will not be here one day to explain. I want to know I tried to warn somebody."

Parvati did not realize how prophetic her words were.

She walked to her bookshelf, which was filled with books in a foreign language and alphabet. It was one of the first times that I realized the whole world didn't use our alphabet. I marveled at the incredible richness of knowing different scriptural systems and the intelligence it required.

"This is Sanskrit," she said. "As a Sudra, I was not allowed to learn Sanskrit or read the Vedas—not as a member of the lowest caste and certainly not as a woman. I will translate a number of sentences. Listen. 'Black skin is impious.' 'The nature of woman is like that of a hyena.' 'Let a female child be born somewhere else; let a male child be born here.'"

"That sure sounds a bit unfriendly," I said.

"But these are our most religious writings, justifying that when a Brahman walks in the shadow of a Dalit they are polluted and must purify themselves with holy water from the Ganges. That is my culture. Look here—Indra, a Vedic god, is thanked because 'he scattered those coming from a black womb.' There are so many hateful references to black skin it makes me sick. Here again: 'The black skin is spewed out of the heavens; the white friends are given the fields, the sun, the waters…'"

Parvati kept going, faster, and faster, through the Vedas. Many parts were highlighted.

"Do you know that the different castes correspond to different colors? The Brahmans, the highest caste, are represented by white—the Sudras, as the lowest beings, by black. In your society, white corresponds with purity, black with evil. Where do you think that comes from?"

I sat in silence and listened to her hurt. What else could I do? She started walking around the apartment, going through the cabinets in her kitchen, putting different jars on the table. I thought she was preparing for her breakfast the next morning. I remember a big pot of honey. Her family had sent it from India. She had always poured a lot of honey in her tea. I used to joke about her sweet tooth. A kettle of water was heated. She had no shower in her room, so that was how she cleaned herself.

All of a sudden, she looked in my direction. "I need you to go now."

I was a bit disappointed; I had hoped I might spend the night with her. I did not insist.

I left her room just after midnight, kissing her softly on the lips. As always, a flash of lust spread through my body when I kissed her. At the door, she pushed a book into my hands. I had given it to her a week before and asked her to read it. "Thanks for lending this to me; I liked it a lot," she whispered. I would never again sleep with her. She died a few hours later.

Chapter 7

Fuengirola: Ugly Dreams

Spain, 1992

*M*ore than ten years have passed. A decade of life. I thought about Parvati today. I was walking along the Paseo Maritimo in Fuengirola, and warm sirocco winds blew fine sand from the African coast trembling in the distance. Sirocco winds speak with a soft voice; they do not roar, they whisper. They murmur memories of love, forgotten and remembered, family, and broken hearts. They whisper the rhythms of Africa. I had not returned to Belgium since leaving. I had no desire to. My family came to see me whenever they felt the need, and I was happy to be left alone. I lived close to the sea and could hear her at night. She soothed me. It took me a while to settle in one place when I left after Parvati's death, but after some months, I settled in the

far southern tip of Europe. And with the help of the
hypnotic sounds of the sea, I managed to sleep better at
night. I sometimes even forgot about the horrible way
Parvati had died.

I avoided contact with other people as much as I
could—not that I was unfriendly—I managed a smile
when they spoke to me, but I avoided answering personal questions. The Costa del Sol is a great place to
avoid answering questions. Petty and white-collar
criminals and victims of costly divorces all mingle on
the coast, where secrets are the common denominator.
Everybody has one. Everybody has something to hide. I
had a tragedy and a bad dream to hide. It took a long
time to verbalize the dream. Not from a lack of words—
I just forgot it every time I woke up. Continued attempts
to remember it eventually paid off.

I am in the middle of the woods. It is dark. Streaks
of shadow and light are cast between the trees. Fog sur-
rounds me. I am not alone. A man is with me. He has a
spade. I am warmly dressed in a heavy jacket, a scarf
around my neck. I look at the man digging a hole. He
digs deeper and deeper. He ignores me. We put a body
in the hole. The body is covered and taped. It looks like
a mummy. I think the man is my father. I wake up and
feel terrible. It all seems so real. Whom did we bury?

The dream kept repeating itself. The anxiety I felt
upon waking became so intense that I enlisted the help
of a dream therapist whose office was in the little church
square in the middle of Fuengirola. She was Danish; her

name was Maya. She was very attractive. After listening to my story and dream, she decided to hypnotize me and search my childhood for traumatic experiences. "Everybody can be hypnotized, but you have to want it," she said confidently. She was never able to hypnotize me, so she decided to use a hallucinatory drug.

When I woke up, Maya was sitting on top of me, holding me closely; my body was united with hers in a tight embrace, rocking forward and backward. She looked at me through a veil and said she had awoken Kundalini, a serpent coiled around the base of my spine, the source of spiritual knowledge and mystical visions. She told me that all physical things and mental constructions were illusions she would unveil. Maya told me that her body, her beauty, and our touch were but illusions, not to be mistaken for the truth. She told me she tried to awaken me to the fact that nothing on earth would ever satisfy my human needs. I remember thinking she was doing a good job satisfying some of my needs. Her breasts were beautiful and pressed willingly against my chest.

"All is illusion; all suffering is illusion," she kept muttering. She asked me to tell her that her body left me indifferent. I could not say that. Maya was a beautiful woman, and she aroused me terribly. I wanted to make love to her.

"You must be hallucinating a lot not to see the suffering in this world," I said.

She pushed herself off me and stood up. She looked at me, defeated and tired.

"I want you to go," she said. "I want you to go now," she repeated harshly.

I asked why she wanted me to go so suddenly. She pushed me out the door, hastily and forcefully.

Just before she slammed the door in my face, she said, "I tried to unveil truth to you. I failed. You do not want to see it. Get out of here. You already know too much, and yet, you know nothing."

I looked at her. She did not make sense.

Before I could say anything, she whispered, "You talk a lot in your sleep. I know all there is to know about you. You never should have met Parvati." Then she slammed the door. I would never meet her again.

I was working for a hotel company in those days. The next day, my manager called me in. A place had opened up in the construction division of the company. Goa had been selected for some new hotel projects. I would be based in the headquarters in Bombay, and later on at sites in Goa. I never had that awful dream again, but I did not find peace. A veil would be lifted, but not the veil of Maya.

Chapter 8

Orissa: A Visit to the Temples

India, 1997

I had been in India for just over four years. I had spent
the bulk of my time in Goa, finalizing construction of
a number of hotels. Goa has kilometer-long beaches and
a promising tourist industry. Around 1997, large numbers of English tourists arrived on direct flights from
Heathrow to Goa. They landed at the military airport,
where they were politely told not to take pictures because of the military nature of the site. The vigor with
which the Indian military imposed the ban on pictures
was farcical, since all there was to see were old struc-
tures filled with outdated jets of Russian origin—a
reminder of the flirtations India had with Soviet social-
ism. For support, they had never looked to Communist
China. China was the only country that stood in the way

of India's goal of being the most populated and potentially most powerful country in the world. Although Pakistan was viewed as an aggressor, most Indians shrugged it off, knowing that if they really wanted they could obliterate that country in a flash. They had more people to mobilize. China was the real threat, the real competition—militarily and economically. Fernandez, a Goan who would become Minister of Defense in later years, repeatedly stressed this point.

Goa was a Portuguese colony until 1961. Evidence of this was everywhere—the Catholic beliefs of half the population, the churches and colonial houses built by them, the public buildings in Goa full of furniture from colonial times, and Portuguese words plastered all over public buildings. The older generation still spoke Portuguese to each other; it was a sign of education and class.

The Churchill brothers were infamous in Goa. They were the law outside the law and had a local football team. When the Churchill brothers attracted skilled black players for their team, the team grew in popularity. They played a naïve kind of soccer, but with a lot of heart. Goans love football. People are always playing soccer somewhere. The brothers were representative of the independent streak all Goans possess.

The Churchills were part of a movement to make Goa a free port and develop it into a gambling paradise. The stories of their exploits were much like their ideas—larger than life. They succeeded with their football team, which was called The Churchill Brothers. It is still one of the best-known teams in India.

Fado, traditional Portuguese music, was a big hit here. At various bars around the Goan beaches, skilled musicians strummed their guitars, singing sad, beautiful songs in the moonlight.

My contact for the company was a local named Thomas, a polite, educated man, proud of his Portuguese roots, so apparent in his last name—Bothello.

Without him, I never would have survived. In this culture, respect for others is not the only quality you need to function and work. You have to understand the local habits. Thomas' help was crucial.

One morning, Thomas knocked on my door at the boarding house in Colva, where I was staying. Colva is a little fishing community beside the sea. The boarding house was small and functional. Beside it was a small farm, and the sounds of animals usually woke me every morning. But this morning, Thomas woke me up and explained that work at the hotel we were constructing for the company had stopped. A snake living in a large Banyan tree at the construction site had shown his head and threatened the workers, just when they wanted to cut the tree. The workers ran from the construction site, saying that the snake was the protector of the tree and the land, and its sighting was a sign that the gods were not happy with our trying to cut down the tree.

I was not very understanding. I shouted, "Cut down the damn tree and kill the snake! We cannot lose more time. We are behind schedule, as it is."

Thomas didn't say a word. I got dressed and went to a small teahouse with him. Thomas talked to me very calmly.

"Jan, you cannot cut the tree down. No one would ever work for us again. I already called a Hindu priest who will bless the land and appease the snake. He will come tomorrow. We will lose a couple of hours, but we'll keep the relationship with our workers intact."

The next day, Thomas and I arrived early in Baga, North Goa, where the construction was taking place, and we waited with the construction crew for the priest. When I say construction crew, you must not imagine a group of skilled men with tools. The construction crew was an assembly of women, children, and old men, the cheapest available labor. Pouring concrete was a skillful division of work. The old men commanded, the children filled pans with handmade concrete, and the women balanced the pots on their heads and moved like spiders over bamboo poles to where the concrete had to go.

Most of the women belonged to nomadic groups from the Rajasthan area, wearing heavy jewelry in their ears and nose. They covered their heads and wore a ghagra skirt and the kanchili—a short sleeved garment worn over the upper part of the body leaving the back bare, barely hiding the female form, but setting the imagination on fire. The effect was not lost on adventurous Western designers, who in later years turned these garments into a must-have for the fashion conscious, but with a Western twist. The women hurling concrete and stones never realized how they influenced the fashion sense of the West with their traditional clothing and bare body parts.

When the priest and his entourage arrived, the site fell silent. The priest looked at the tree where the snake was seen and an improvised shrine had been built.

"Do not worry," Thomas whispered in my ear. "The outcome is assured. I promised him a nice sum to make sure the snake allows us to cut down the tree and build here."

But things in India never work out as one thinks they will. Suddenly, the priest turned around and left. Thomas followed him. Half a day later, Thomas returned. The priest had gone straight to a Hindu temple and placed some leaves on a statue of a Hindu god. Then he had entered a kind of trance and started asking the statue questions. The priest's questions were answered by whether leaves fell from the statue or not. There was either a fallen leaf or a leaf that refused to fall. Thomas was never clear about that, but it had been a negative sign. The priest was adamant; the tree should not be cut. He kept the money Thomas gave him.

The tree was never cut down. We moved the building by two meters and kept the tree, the peace, and the workers. The tree is now an attraction and can be seen by all who visit Monte Rio in Baga.

After that episode, Thomas and I became friends. We needed a rest, so we visited the temples in Bhubaneswar, Orissa, at Thomas' insistence. During our train trip, Thomas told me a lot about Orissa. His daughter was studying anthropology and doing an extensive study on the tribes in this province, at the Bay of Bengal. That, he confessed, was one of the reasons he wanted to take me there. I did not mind. I liked the adventure.

"Kondh, Bondas, Santals, Juangs, Parajas, Oraon, Godabas, and Koyas—did you ever hear of these tribes? Many still lead a simple life. Hunting and agriculture are how they survive." It was clear that Thomas admired these people.

"They ignore development programs from the Indian government and the World Bank. They refuse to be introduced to modern times. It is believed there are over sixty tribes with traditions and customs predating the invasion of the Aryans."

That attracted my attention. I had been in India long enough and had heard enough over the years to know that that sort of reference was politically loaded. Many years had passed since that fateful night when Professor Kumar insisted there were no pre-Aryan times. The Hindu culture had not grown from barbaric invaders. The Aryans had always been there; they were the original inhabitants. Indian magazines had long, feuding discussions about the origins of the Aryan population. Right-wing Hindu magazines aggressively defended the stand that Aryans were the original inhabitants. Magazines with a different orientation kept to the "barbaric invader" theories.

Three years had passed since the bomb attacks in Bombay. Hindus were developing a new sensitivity, and the BJP, capitalizing on this, was challenging the once invincible Congress Party for control of India. Thomas, however, was a Christian and more open to the exotic past of the Indian subcontinent.

"My daughter told me about dormitory life among the Bonda," Thomas continued. "It is playful and, I suppose, decadent to our sensitive ears. Unmarried boys and girls meet each other, unsupervised, in dorms—dancing, touching, and exploring each other in the most intimate ways. The hope is that this develops into a marriage. I admire the atmosphere of adolescent naïveté created for the young to meet and find a life partner. It is a far cry from the arranged marriages of my country, where caste and dowry are the most powerful determinations for your life partner."

Thomas looked at me with a big smile; this father and devoted husband felt a sensuality for life that I had not seen before.

Bhubaneswar, the capital of Orissa, is a metropolis for Indian temples. It was rumored that once there were more than seven thousand of them. Now, there are only five hundred left. When we arrived, the temples dominating the Bhubaneswar landscape overwhelmed me. It was an architectural feat on a par with the greatest architectural achievements of man, but it did not end there. When we visited the temples, I noticed that an overwhelming number of skillful sculptures filled the walls of the temples—many of an explicit, sexual nature.

For me, the Kama Sutra was the epiphany of sexual liberation and liberty. I never understood how a sexually conservative society could have produced such an exquisitely sensual work. I have seen the pictures in the Kama Sutra. The pictures make it a great read. Naively, not based on any real insight, I believed the Kama Sutra was the origin of sensuality and sexuality in India, and that any sexual picture or text could be traced back to this book.

So my first reaction, when I saw the Lingaraj temple with its masterful depictions of birds, beasts, and men and women in erotic positions, was to tell Thomas how I admired the creative source the Kama Sutra was for Indian culture. He nodded, but in a peculiar Indian way—his head bobbing from left to right, not agreeing or disagreeing. I did not push my point further; we were entering the temple, confronted by the phallic symbol of Shiva, in all his majesty. Thomas and I visited many more temples—the Rajarani temple, Luxmaneswar, Satrughaneswar and Bharteswar, Parsurameswar and Swarna Jaleswar, Vaital, Mukteswar, and Anant Basudeva. In every temple, we were confronted with explicitly sexual scenes covering the range of human sexuality. Some scenes turned me on; some were obscene and affronted my sense of decency, which was peculiar, as I saw myself as liberated, open-minded.

On one of the temple visits, I started talking to a tourist. Soon, our conversation turned to the many erotic scenes with which we were confronted. He expressed surprise that a conservative society like India, where arranged marriages were the norm and bodies were covered from top to toe in saris, had such a liberated sculptural tradition.

He pointedly asked, "How did these Kama Sutra sculptures survive the Victorian tastes of the English Raj and conservative Indian society?" It was a rhetorical question, but he left me wondering about the answer.

"Kama Sutra sculptures? Where do you people hear that nonsense?" somebody, a man with long strands of dirty hair covering his face and wide-open eyes, shouted in my ear, interrupting my musings. He was one of the many holy men wandering the temples, and he spoke excellent English. He also could not leave his crotch alone and scratched it constantly.

"Look," he said, "you see these homo and hetero-sexual anal scenes here. This was never mentioned in the Kama Sutra. Bestiality was never spoken of in the Kama Sutra, but you find it all over the temples. Numerous theories have been developed regarding the scenes depicted here, designed to hide the truth. People are afraid of explicit sexual scenes—women having sexual congress with deer and dogs. They misunderstand men measuring their phallus, offering semen to fire, oral sex, and gay sex.

"The Brahmans had a lot of work to do to cover up the pre-Aryan origins of the sexual scenes. They had to hide pre-Aryan sources of religions as Tantrism and the worship of Shiva, Shaivism. They could not muster the openly sexual, sensual nature of the original inhabitants of India—those who lived here before the Aryans arrived—but traces of the original pre-Hindu religions survived in some places. Today, these monuments stand as testimonies to pre-Aryan religions—defying the small tastes of the Hindus and Brahmans.

"When I was young, I saw the Mahavrata celebration, a fertility festival. The Brahmans tried to incorporate this Shiva celebration by transforming it into a religious festival, stripped of all sexual origin. But in villages today, contrary to Brahman instructions, public coitus under the auspicious eyes of the village does happen. This is how Shiva is celebrated. Sometimes stories are leaked to the press, and then the rituals are called barbaric, deviant expressions of a sick people, but it is merely an expression of India's authentic culture. It is how they rebel, how they hold to their beliefs and say no to the bastardization of those beliefs under a wide Hindu wing."

I stared at him for a moment or two after his outburst and muttered, "Your English is very good."

"For a dirty native—is that what you are thinking? I am English; I have lived here for thirty years and have fun shocking people like you. I have studied the temples in Orissa my whole life. My father was born here, I was born here; I grew up here. I returned as a young man and never left again."

I told him I understood how the Brahmans had perverted the original beliefs of India to further their control of Indian society. I told him I understood that there was a great plan of control for the Hindu religion.

The English holy man look-alike nodded. "You are an intelligent man," he said, mockingly. "You know how much horseshit goes around about these erotic designs? Kama Sutra depiction? Don't make me laugh. The Kama Sutra is a watered-down erotic work to make sexuality accessible and acceptable for the masses and hide a much more explicitly sexual society. The Aryan Brahmans could not control a society of people indulging in orgiastic feasts and enjoying themselves. They needed to control it, so they twisted it into acceptable creative forms. Their authority challenged, they embraced the opposition, absorbed their ideas, and incorporated them."

"Like the Jains and the Buddhists," I whispered.

He heard me. "Yes, like them. A challenge to Brahman authority, they were embraced, and then marginalized, and now only fringe movements exist in India. Shaivism, Tantrism, Shaktism—old pre-Aryan religions—they are watered-down to fit the house of Hinduism. Open sexuality was a grave threat to Brahman authority. Sexual and erotic pleasure was a force that would challenge any authority preaching austerity in this life to have a better next life. People who enjoy their bodies uninhibitedly cannot be controlled. They do not need an afterlife. They enjoy it here and are not concerned with working on their karma. They no longer accept the authority of holy books and priests. Therefore, instead of confronting sexuality and sensuality, the Brahmans accepted it, but watered it down over the ages, and see where we are today. The Kama Sutra is marginalized in India. AIDS is on the rise because nobody can even talk about people as sexual beings. The Brahmans have absolute control; they have created an asexual society. Pure sensual reality challenges every earthly control men try to impose on each other. They want to keep sensuality and sexuality at bay."

I was not sure if the chronic scratching of his genital area had a non-verbal meaning. I stared at his busy hands. Here was a man lecturing me on philosophy and religion, wearing rags on his body, and dealing with a very itchy crotch. His arguments had a flawless rationale and were delivered with intelligence, but were undermined by his rag-doll appearance and poor body language. He must have been aware of my aversion, but it did not stop him from continuing his lecture. I suspect my discomfort actually amused him. He continued to talk while I stared at his hands.

"Hinduism, the one belief open for all others. That is one of the biggest frauds in modern history. To explain these sexual scenes in the temples, which prove ties to pre-Aryan religions and remind people of a time they were not controlled by Brahmans, Brahman scholars came up with wild stories. Some said the erotic scenes were encouraged by local kings to ensure a high reproduction rate, to ensure replacements for deceased soldiers. Ridiculous. How bestiality and sodomy help increase reproduction is beyond me. One anthropologist likened the erotic scenes to a giant comic strip carved in stone to provide sex education to the population cheaply—as if people needed sexual education!

"Other scientists believe these sculptures were a marketing tool to attract pilgrims from far and beyond, so as to increase the revenue for the king, since all pilgrims were obliged to contribute to the king's coffers. How men fondling female organs would increase the flow of devout pilgrims is so farfetched, it does not even deserve consideration. That it now functions as a great marketing tool to attract tourists is beyond doubt, though. Still others have claimed the carvings were tests for the virtue of pilgrims—a test of the strength of one's character over the hormonal-driven desires that live in all of us. Then why would some of the scenes be hidden, almost impossible to find? Why would it show aristocrats masturbating?

"Hinduism projects itself as an inclusive black hole, a force of nature, attracting people of good will looking for salvation and God. It does so without claiming a monopoly on salvation. Once you become one with God, you attain salvation. In Hinduism, an atheist, a Muslim, a Jew, a Christian, or a Buddhist can attain salvation. Anybody searching for truth is a Hindu. There is one truth; men just describe it in different ways."

Thomas nodded in agreement. He had stood beside me the whole time in silence.

"But," I interjected, "if all can be integrated under one banner of truth and tolerance, why the religious violence in India?"

The English holy man looked at me and said, "Ask yourself another question: Why, in this realm of tolerance, is there no place for explicit sexuality? Why did the Brahmans and Hinduism have to jump through hoops to justify the sexual depictions surrounding us? Why was there no place for certain ways of life or thinkers like Charvaka? What are they protecting? Answer that, and then you will find an answer to your question."

Again that name! I stared at him with wide eyes. Why would he mention Charvaka? Charvaka appeared repeatedly in my life, an evil avatar, reminding me of the one true tragedy in my life.

The holy man continued, "Why are the Brahmans so scared, if their beliefs are tolerant and welcome dissent?"

As quickly as he had appeared, the English native disappeared, leaving Thomas and me pondering what he had said. I mainly remembered Charvaka's name. It had disappeared from the pages of history, but it was a recurrent virus in my life.

Thomas and I left the temple. I was still thinking over what I had heard when Thomas grasped my shirt-sleeve and pulled me toward a car he had stopped with wild hand gestures. It was a small minivan; he opened the sliding door and both of us fell, tired and sweaty, into the back seat. On our way back to the hostel where we were staying, we followed a wide, four-lane road split by a concrete barrier.

We were exhausted from our temple visits as our holiday ended, so we leaned back and closed our eyes, glad for a rest. I thought about how Charvaka had reappeared in my life. Suddenly, the driver let out a loud shriek. Thomas and I opened our eyes just as a loud noise on the right side of the car indicated we had hit something. We shouted at the driver to stop, but he ignored us and drove on. We pulled at his shoulder to force him to stop, but he pulled a piece of wood from under his seat and started swinging at us.

As if by divine intervention, his front wheel exploded. The abrupt increase in speed as he sped away from the collision had been too much for his old tires. He stopped the minivan, opened his door, and ran away, leaving Thomas and me behind. We pushed the car from the road and retraced our steps. It took only a few minutes to find a young man with a broken, bloody leg lying on the road. Cars passed, but nobody stopped.

We started tending to the young man and stopped another minivan. At first, the driver refused to take the man to a hospital, afraid the blood would sully his car seats. When I pointed out that they were dirty already, he stared at me with blank eyes. I pulled out a wad of bills, and the reluctant driver immediately became helpful. There was only room enough for the wounded man in the van, not for us. The driver promised to bring him to the nearest hospital. Thomas and I had to stop another van to get back to our hostel.

That night I sat with Thomas in a little local roadside restaurant in Bhubaneswar, just beside our hostel. We were eating rotis and dahl and enjoying it very much. We did not discuss the incident that had occurred earlier on the road. We never asked ourselves whether the man really reached the hospital. We never discussed our fear that the driver may not have delivered the wounded man as promised. We never asked if we had done enough. We never wondered why the guilty driver ran away—justice could be harsh in India and not always lawful. We were in survival mode. We talked, however. We talked a lot.

We contemplated what we had heard and seen over the last couple of days. I asked Thomas why the Brahmans and Hinduism seemed to seize all religious and philosophical thinking. The soft-spoken Christian from Goa looked a bit sad.

"History is the story of the Brahmans and their quest for power," he said with defiant acceptance. "Even today, they are rewriting history! We are only a step away from believing Hindus, not Muslims, built the Taj Mahal. A barrage of stories tells us there was never an invasion of Aryans—that no one lived here before the Aryans. Sophisticated theories explain that there was neither an Aryan population nor a separate Dravidian population, although archeological research proves otherwise. They want us to believe that Brahmans cannot be descended from barbarians. India is the ancestral land of Hindus and Hinduism; its culture and religion cannot be born of barbaric invaders. The Brahmans have always decided history and the course of Hinduism. Have you heard about the Vedas and Manu, the great sage?"

I nodded.

"It is ironic that the racist theories of the West can be traced back to the chauvinism of the Aryans millennia ago on the Indian subcontinent. The epicenter of knowledge in Indian society, the origin of many great religions, possessing a deep spiritual fabric, is no more than a crude instrument to categorize and enslave people. When the Nazis and right-wing idiots in the West use race as a mark of distinction, they had better remember we, Indians, are at the base of it all. Indian Aryans as founders of racism? What would white supremacists think of that?

"The Vedas and Brahmans made their influence felt in the world. When the English were in charge of India, they were confounded by the enormous diversity of religions. In the 17th century, the English controlled India militarily, but the Brahmans controlled the social fabric of most of the Indian subcontinent, as they had done for centuries. Sure, there was some dissent, most notably Buddhists turned against the caste system; they were absorbed and became innocent fringe movements, but people are inventive, and India is enormous. In all corners of India, pre-Aryan-tribes and religions survived.

After centuries of Brahman power, some people still resisted their rule, their version of religion, to the Brahmans' great dismay.

"The English did not want to administer such a diversity of religions. It would result in a very ineffective bureaucracy. They invented the myth of Hinduism, Sanatana Dharma, or Righteousness Forever, the myth of one Indian religion. The Brahman elites, who helped rule this vast continent, whispered it in their ears. Hinduism became the cover for all religions, the national religion. The English invented Hinduism as a mono-theology. The Brahmans liked that very much. The oppressor was doing their work for them, uniting a diverse and unmanageable country. The English brought movements, tribes, and religions still free of Brahman powers under control.

"The English were looking for a legal basis to create a centralized powerbase. One of their scholars, William Jones, started translating the writings of Manu. He was brought up in the European tradition, in which a body of law, derived from biblical principles, guided society. He looked for a fundamental religious text to use as the basis for an Indian body of law. But Indian society was organized according to local communities' own customs and traditions. Pandits interpreted old religious texts according to their personal insights and hundreds of possible and respected interpretations. For the English, it was immensely frustrating to hear pandits in similar situations rule differently. The English were determined to find a base for law, and the Brahman elite were happy to help them create a uniform code. At their suggestion, Manu and the poisonous thoughts of the Vedas started entering the world. If you've heard of Manu, you know he's a real piece of work."

"I know, Thomas. He's contemptible. I heard about him through somebody I met a couple years ago, an American scholar who told me pretty much the same story, including a lot about Manu and his theories."

"There is even a statue of William Jones with the writings of Manu in his hand in St. Paul's Cathedral in London. Racism has Vedic origins, and this is where it comes from. Once the writings of Manu were translated into English, they were translated quickly into German, French, and Portuguese. The European Orientalists really thought this work was the highest expression of Hindu culture and thought. Brahmans made sure the English were fed with this illusion and thus supported the implementation of Manu's laws. The English naively taught they were merely imposing laws by which the Hindus were governed, anyway. It was a cunning move.

"The English destroyed a complex system of dynamic and creative self-governance that guided the workings of local communities, and the Brahmans, with the book of Manu in their hands, stood by as victors, their superiority enshrined in law. For thousands of years, the Brahman caste had tried to create an Indian nation, but failed, and then the English did it for them.

Soon the Brahmans turned on the hand that had fed them and kicked the English out."

Thomas gave me a little smile when he finished. The next day, we returned to Goa. I had to find out who Charvaka was, but he remained but a whisper, an illusion of promise, and the key to a web of age-old conspiracies. How could I find out more?

Little did I know that Parvati would speak to me from beyond her grave and show me the world of Charvaka.

Chapter 9

Charvaka

A few months ago

*L*ife is not a story. It is not a chronicle of events with a beginning, middle, and end. That is what we make of it; we cling to an idea of order, fulfilling a demand hard-wired into our genes to find some sense. We merely experience things, a superficial process, ephemeral, backed up by a failing memory with glitches and viruses. Our experiences we connect; we associate, sometimes. Those connections and associations lead to certain insights. We can try to share the connections, but there is no guarantee that we'll uncover the same insights.

We are subjected to endless streams of information. Facts or truths are no longer relevant. We use information, in part and whimsically, regardless of validity or moral relevance. Type any two words into a search engine on the Internet, and a connection will appear.

Anybody can make a story, share it, but that is no guarantee of a conclusion.

Previous chapters may have given the impression that Charvaka was the key to a dreadful secret—the last chapter in a book that would clarify all previous events.

Understanding Charvaka will clarify some events and lead to distressing insights, but only if you want to understand. That is true for every argument. There is always a belief factor, which may be the only factor, once all is said and done. Few understand the consequences of non-locality in the field of quantum physics or the qualities of light, so mere mortals like us are consigned to believing, not necessarily understanding.

The most disturbing realization one can make is that, as the body of human knowledge grows, we understand less, believe more, and we are more easily subjected to manipulation. Skepticism is probably a healthy attitude in these circumstances, however counterproductive it may be.

A month had passed since I received disturbing news during a call to my father. He had tried to locate me for days, sent me e-mails, but to no avail. I was trekking along the Cambodian border, taking a break from work in India, to locate friends of mine on a holiday there. He had sad news for me. My mother had passed away. I knew she was sick—cancer had eaten at her for years. She had done better lately. I chatted with her whenever I could, and in the last couple of weeks, she had sounded much more alive. When my father told me of her death,

I was devastated. I was not there with him. I had not been there when my mother passed away. I flew back the next day.

After my mother's funeral, I helped my father clean the house they lived in, the house where I grew up. We packed my mother's clothes and locked them in old suitcases in the attic. When I was in the attic, I discovered a box with my old textbooks and notes. When I left the university in Leuven, I had dropped off my books and notes at home with my father. I remembered how disappointed he looked the day he realized I would not finish my studies, but he understood the tragedy I was involved in and never blamed me for my decision. I had always admired him for that and was grateful.

The box had not been opened for more than two decades. I opened it and started browsing through my old course notes. I hardly recognized my writing. We constantly evolve and change, and our handwriting is part of that process. Time had flown, and decades separated me now from my shocking experience with Parvati.

Suddenly, I came across a book in the middle of my course materials—*Death in Midsummer and Other Stories*, by Mishima. When I was younger, I had been very intrigued by the Japanese homosexual latter-day warrior who committed seppuku in public, surrounded by friends and followers. With his love for his body and his immensely sensual writings, he personified a warrior-poet that spoke to the boy in me. There are many pictures of Mishima in homoerotic stances showing his muscles, which he slowly built with years of weight training, leaving him a far cry from the young, weak boy that grew up around women.

Then, an envelope fell out of the book. "To Jan," it said. It was yellow, and the glue that was supposed to keep it closed was no longer sticking. I took the papers out and looked at the first page. It was written in Parvati's handwriting and bore her signature. I had never seen it before. She must have sneaked it into the book on the last night I saw her alive. I had given the book to her to read, and she gave it back to me the night she died. The next day, I was informed of her murder and taken to the police station. I never looked at my course materials or books again.

The papers I give you, Jan, are all that is left of Charvaka. It is more than ever necessary in my country, India, that his ideas survive. It is my family's duty to see to it. His ideas are immense in their kindness and representation of the common man. They tell us to question, enjoy, and tolerate. He tolerated us; this most atheist of atheists, this most materialist of materialists, accepted us—our religion, ceremonies, deities, and joyous views of life. His tolerance and erudition so threatened the status quo and the Brahmans that they made him disappear. They are succeeding, bit by bit, Jan; I can no longer ensure he survives.

Parvati had signed the handwritten note with her name. There was a postscript.

They are close now, Jan. Please, help me preserve Charvaka. Read these papers, and bring them to my aunt—Sumathi Dhanji in Bangkok.

A detailed address followed.

I looked up in shock. After the death of my mother, Parvati and all the horrible memories associated with her came to haunt me once again. I looked at the papers she had given me for safekeeping.

They were entries, randomly printed remarks—all written in what I supposed was Sanskrit. The letters were beautifully formed and had a very abstract quality. Interjected into the text were written remarks that I supposed were from Parvati, for again, I recognized her handwriting.

Carvaka or Charvaka, also known as Lokayata: atheist of the materialist school of thought, which can be traced back as far as the 5th century BC and even further, to the Vedas. Brahmanical opponents have destroyed this philosophy. The principal ideas of Charvaka are gathered from fragments cited by Hindu, Jain, and Buddhist opponents.

Why does the West teach that materialism and freethinking are their ideas? Am I to believe that the "Enlightenment," the breakthrough of human intellect as is projected in every European university, is the highway to freethinking, rational thoughts and humanism? Do they really believe that the world was repressed before European enlightened thinkers came along to rescue it? Sheer arrogance. Free thought and materialism are engraved in our genes.

I browsed further through the papers and found what looked like a poem that was attributed to Charvaka by Parvati:

Yavajjivet sukham jivet |
Rinam kritvaa ghritam pibet ||
Bhasmibhutasya dehasya |
Punaraagamanam kutah ||

As long as you live happily, take a loan and drink ghee. After a body is reduced to ashes, where will it come back from?

I looked with amazement at the Indian variation of "Eat, drink, and be merry, for tomorrow we die." This hedonistic insight must be centuries older.

The irony of the situation did not escape me. To be confronted with these ideas just after having buried your mother did not strike me as the best way to mourn. Having seen my mother's body cold and hard in the hospital ward, melted away by disease, I hoped she had gone to a better place, but the absurdity of these thoughts struck me immediately. Older, wiser men had thought the same. It does not coincide with the picture of India as a land of spiritual seekers in pursuit of a better self, but the quote was real.

A bit further on, Parvati referred to a work I had heard about on my travels. *The Sarvadarsanasangraha* by Madhavacharya. This 14th century book, its title almost impossible to pronounce, would most certainly not be on any bestseller list, but it is widely regarded in India.

The Sarvadarsanasangraha is the primary source of what we know about Charvaka. Written in the 14th century AD, it has numerous references regarding Charvaka. The purpose of the quotes attributed to Charvaka is to refute his thoughts.

Then followed more inserts in English from Parvati. They were, I thought, translations or comments between the rows of Sanskrit writing.

There is no heaven, no final liberation, or soul in another world.

The only eternal entity is matter—earth, water, fire, and air. Life and intelligence grow out of these four elements alone. With death ends all. Life originates from inanimate substance.

If sacrificed animals go to heaven, why don't you sacrifice your father and send him to heaven with sacrificial rites?

If he who departs from the body goes to another world, how is it that he does not come back again, restless for the love of his family?

The ceremonies for the dead were established so Brahmans could live a life of luxury.

The authors of the Vedas were buffoons, knaves, and demons.

These obscene rites—they were invented by buffoons.

More of Parvati's scribbles followed—the same anti-clerical, anti-Brahman vitriol. I started understanding why Charvaka and his followers were so hated. They were really kicking the establishment's legs. Central Hindu themes of rebirth, salvation, and living in heaven after death were rejected in quote after quote as utter nonsense—centuries before the birth of Christ. Charvaka and his followers undermined the cozy life the Brahmans led. Resentment must have been huge. Was it enough to make him disappear from the pages of history? Was it enough to explain murder, hundreds of years later in Belgium? Was it enough to explain Jay's accusation of the Jains for the bomb attack in Bombay?

Parvati wrote more:

The Sarvadarsanasangraha quotes the Charvaka philosophies to refute and destroy them. The Brahmans needed to. If there are no such things as a soul, rebirth, and salvation, materialism and carpe diem should be considered the right path, the only path by which to lead your life. There would be no purpose to spiritual quests. Karma would have no basis. Enjoy life while you can; once you are cremated, there is no return. Charvaka showed how man, with the invention of God, shackled himself to ideas of heaven and hell, becoming incapable of taking destiny into his own hands. Charvaka was very popular among the common people—so popular the Brahmans had to destroy him; they feared the common people would stop paying tribute to them and their priests. What would happen if the common people no longer obeyed them? What if they lost their fear of punishment in the next life for sins committed in this one?

More followed, and it seemed important; everything else she wrote was heavily underlined.

It was a cheap shot to portray Charvaka as an opportunistic hedonist, not that this aspect was not important, but what bugged the Brahmans was his rejection of the Vedas.

The scene between Professor Kumar and Parvati came back to mind. She had rattled his cage intensely, and now I could see why. She, by invoking the name of Charvaka, had questioned the basis of Indian society and his beliefs. She had invoked a name very few knew, whose existence was a threat to Brahmans and what they stood for.

Even more dangerous than the rejection of the Vedas, the castes, and the prevalent position of the Brahmans was Charvaka's popularity among the common people. Charvaka, with his belief in the reality of the world and the physical existence of man on earth, and nothing else, was a blessing for the common people. He rejected heaven and hell, good and bad. Charvaka and his followers were smart and alluring. Some believed Charvaka should be translated as a charming, sweet speaker. They were good orators. Common folk loved them. They rejected the speculative metaphysics of the Vedas, believing in direct perception to interact with the world. The fact that they stressed joyful living helped their popularity, too. The Buddhist and Jains, with their stress on penance, had a marketing problem. Compared to Charvaka, they were boring, joyless creatures. The hell with them.

Charvaka rejected the humbug about castes and high and low status. Don't all organs in the human body have the same value? None is more important than another. Charvaka and his followers rejected the castes in simple, direct language. They attacked authority and led sensual lives. There were no metaphysical musings of holy men starving themselves to death. Who could connect with that?

Getting rich and passion were postulated as goals to pursue. This was something everybody could understand. Charvaka saw men and women on an equal footing. All this meant that this most popular of thinkers had to be taken down in a manner unprecedented in history. A pact with the devil was made. Not only did the Brahmans turn against him, so did other adversaries of the Brahmans—the Jains and the Buddhists. The outcome was deadly for Charvaka.

After more then two decades, I understood more about the motives behind Parvati's death. She had been dangerous to a religious order that was millennia old. She had been dangerous to the picture Mother India had projected for thousands of years—a land of spiritual quests and the origin of some of the most admired religions in the world. She denied a belief in the afterlife and put her own pleasure ahead of piety.

God, sex had been good with her!

She was a descendent of a line of people who dared question, who took another point of view, who lived and loved as freely, but how did it tie in with the way she was murdered? I decided to go to Bangkok—to the aunt she had named—and look for clarification. There were many papers here, but most I could neither read nor understand. I did not want to involve anybody in my own country because of my connection to Parvati's murder case, and I did not want to drag my father into this. I wanted to leave, now that I had put my mother to rest.

Chapter 10

Bangkok

Very recently

I knocked carefully at the door. I was nervous. The city was hectic and full of traffic. What else is there to say about Bangkok, the melting pot of Thai, Chinese, and Indian culture? There were many reasons to come to this town, some good, and some bad. I was looking for Sumathi Dhanji, Parvati's aunt, not knowing if she would still live at an address more than twenty years old, passed to me by Parvati from beyond the grave.

She did not.

The new owner of the house could tell me where she lived, however. Everybody knew her; she was apparently the major shareholder in the biggest publicly traded property fund in Thailand. He gave me a number to call.

I called immediately. A man who identified himself as the housekeeper answered the phone and told me Sumathi Dhanji was not home. I left a message stating that

I was a friend of her niece Parvati and wanted to speak to her. I hoped her curiosity would be aroused enough to contact me.

I was right. At nine o'clock at night, the phone rang.

"You are more than twenty years too late, Jan!"

She knew my name? I had not left my name for her. How did she know my name?

She asked how I was and if my trip had been comfortable. She spoke to me like a long lost friend, somebody she knew. Her friendliness was overwhelming and strange.

Then she said, "We need to meet."

I agreed, and she asked me to go to the lobby of the hotel where I was staying. She would send her driver to pick me up. I hung up the phone and stared at it for a long time. Questions flooded my head. I had expected to see Parvati's aunt, but I had not expected it would be that easy and quick. I was relieved it had gone so smoothly. Maybe I would be able to have some closure in Parvati's death. I certainly hoped so.

The driver brought me to a large compound on Sathorn road. Sumathi Dhanji was clearly a very successful woman. When the front door of her house was opened, a friendly staff member directed me to a large sitting room, where tea and sweets were served. Then Sumathi Dhanji entered the room. I stood up and stopped breathing when she walked in. She was beautiful end elegant. She had the same features as Parvati. Despite the age difference and the two decades that had passed, the resemblance was unmistakable. It had a greater emotional impact on me than I expected. I showed her the papers that Parvati had left me.

Parvati's aunt wasted no time. She grabbed my hand, forced me gently into a seat, and said, "Drink your tea and listen. What I will tell you, the world needs and will always need. There are many ways to acquire knowledge. Western scientists laugh when told Indian businessmen go to astrologers for advice before contracts are signed. But they accept bank traders' advice, based on arbitrary interpretations of highs and lows and imaginary lines, as if that tells more than the stars in the sky.

"There are those who only believe in what they see and experience. They do not accept that anything can be inferred about the afterlife or metaphysical truth. Not an easy path, but it is a path. Right or wrong, they are necessary in history. Skeptics are found everywhere. They always seem to survive attack. Skeptics, freethinkers, materialists, whatever you want to call them, keep us from excesses—religious or scientific. It is a beautiful example of what we humans are capable. India, especially, treated them very harshly; most of Charvaka's writings were destroyed. He and his followers were attacked and killed.

"In the Hindu epic, *Mahabharata*, a person called Charvaka was burned alive. This is one of the messages that this work, as popular as the Bible or the Koran, contains. It is a clear indication of what India's elite thought

117

of Charvaka. It was a brilliant move. The book was as well liked as soap operas and was a powerful vehicle to denounce Charvaka. It succeeded.

"Charvaka was called a monster and immoral. In other important writings, Charvaka's philosophy is projected as degrading one's character. In the Puranas, it is called a philosophy for the vulgar. But people claimed that as a badge of honor and Charvaka philosophy became known as lokayata—'thinking of the vulgar people' or 'he who believes in the reality of the world.'"

"I never forgot her," I blurted suddenly. "I never fell in love again. I didn't realize how much she meant to me, but I never forgot her. Her death left me alone in the world. I could never love anybody again."

Mrs. Sumathi Dhanji nodded. "I know. We, her family, loved her very much. It killed me when she died, but it did not surprise me. She called me on the last night you saw her. She told me about you and her love for you. She told me how afraid she was to tell you all her secrets and what she stood for. She told me that the same night you encountered the terrible legacies against which the Indian people have to struggle. Parvati told me she was afraid it would drive you away forever."

I was silent as I listened to what Mrs. Sumathi Dhanji had to say. "Do you remember what Parvati told you the night she died? Through extreme ritualism, the Brahmans controlled the people. Aryan superiority, justified by the Vedas, was imposed on us. But never underestimate the people. They reacted, and that reaction came in various forms. The Buddhist believers opposed it, the Jains, too. The Brahmans reviled them all. Those who declared themselves against the rituals prescribed by the Vedas were called the ritual-less people—nastikas. The Brahmans made this a synonym for atheist. Atheism not only became synonymous with somebody who rejected the Vedic rituals, but implied the refusal to admit to the existence of a god, a smart political move designed to turn the masses against movements criticizing the Brahman Vedic truths.

"Charvaka's followers, the Buddhists, and Jains, initially united and defended their ideas together. The Brahmans saw the danger to their supremacy, but also the weakness in the alliance between the Buddhists, Jains, and Charvaka. They started exploiting the weaknesses. The pious life the Jains and Buddhists prescribed was not easily merged with the pursuit of the senses that Charvaka preached. Charvaka's outright rejection of karma and rebirth, and his aggressive stand against the existence of God put him on a collision course with the Jains and Buddhists, who integrated godly concepts more and more. They wanted to avoid being condemned to a footnote on the pages of history by the Brahmans and compromised with the Vedic writings.

"The Brahmans accommodated the Buddhist and Jain movements as much as they could. They became the accepted safe harbors for those who rebelled against the Brahmans, and the Brahmans let it be and accepted their existence. Buddhist and Jain opposition by extremely pious people defused the anger directed toward the Brahman caste. The Brahmans clung to power by accepting institutionalized opposition. They had nothing to fear from people preaching poverty while running around naked or from people who defined life as suffering. If they waited long enough, they knew the people would reconcile themselves to the Vedic truths.

"But Charvaka they could not accept. The Brahmans turned everything and everyone against him. The Buddhist and Jain movements survived and thrived under Brahman acceptance by opposing Charvaka, and their rejection of Charvaka was easily justifiable to their followers, as Charvaka was the fountainhead of a very controversial idea: there is no divine being telling you how to live. Your morals, your ideas of good and bad are the result of social convention. They are manmade constructs to deny our urges. They reject our nature. Increase pleasure in life, soothe your senses, that is where wisdom lies. Charvaka and his followers lived sexually liberated lives, and it irked the Buddhists, Jains, and Brahmans. Even then, sexuality had the power to divide people.

"What really displeased Hindu, Buddhist, and Jain scholars was the iron logic Charvaka and his followers followed. Their belief in perception and rejection of inference—Hobbes and Hume in Indian clothes, if you like—was hard to handle. They rejected beliefs based on the teachings of others, especially the Vedas and their justification of castes. Why were they so hated? They were despicable sophists. They were against everything and everybody. They were against society.

"The real irony is that Charvaka started as somebody searching for knowledge; he decided he would only trust his own perceptions. He asked questions, a most human of attitudes, not that outlandish, even for the Vedas. Brihospoti, the preceptor of all gods, one of the 'rishis' and authors of the Rig Veda, had some pungent questions himself. Brihospoti asked,

Where is God, who has seen him?

Who can confirm that our oblation goes to the supreme God?

How does God protect his followers?

How does the worshipper receive benefit by performing sacrificial rites?

"Brihospoti's were the first materialist questions and led to logic of subjective experience as a basis for everything. Do not believe anything beyond your senses; nothing not personally experienced by you can be trusted.

"From there it was a short journey to the total rejection of God and a Supreme Reason, which can only lead to total rejection of all moral codes. And so, perfectly logical, rational questions led to atheism, materialism, and a revolutionary point of view—vis-à-vis morality. Suddenly, human beings were liberated from arbitrary moral codes. Charvaka, as spearhead of this way of thinking, became a lightning rod, utterly hated by Buddhism, Jainism, and Hinduism alike. It is quite a journey, isn't it?"

"How did the Hindu scholars explain that one of the authors of the Rig Veda questioned the usefulness of rituals and the existence of God the Almighty?" I asked.

"Good question. Scholars explain Brihospoti dealt with these questions as a pre-emptive strike against the hard materialism and skepticism that would confront Vedic metaphysical ideas in the future. He foresaw these cynical attacks and dealt with them before they would become an issue. Hindu thinkers, in later writings, explained Brihospoti's questioning of God and rituals as nonsense taught to a student who was unworthy of his spiritual counsel and knowledge of the Vedas. Brihospoti told the student that the senses and body are all there is. Brihospoti told him there was no meaning in a spiritual quest. The student was sent on his way, lost in the wilderness of the real world with false knowledge. His name was Charvaka. Anybody on a spiritual quest needs to refute Charvaka's premises at the outset. Charvaka followed his senses and preached carpe diem. He feasted on melted butter and lived on the borrowings of friends— not the right mindset for spiritual enlightenment."

I nodded in agreement.

My head was spinning after the flurry of information and clarification. I held my head in my hands and rubbed my temples, first lightly, but then with more pressure as I tried to keep the information I had just received in order by sheer physical effort. When I lifted my head and removed my hands to let Sumathi continue with her story, I saw the driver who had picked me up standing in a corner of the room. He must have been there all the time. The lighting in the room was such that I could hardly detect him. When he picked me up, I had attempted to strike up a conversation with him, but his one-word answers were an obvious indication of an unwillingness to talk. When he turned quite deliberately in the shadows, as if to make sure his presence was known, a corner of his jacket opened up just long enough for me to see he was carrying a gun. I realized he was there to protect Sumathi.

Sumathi followed my gaze. "He has saved my life twice," she said matter-of-factly. "My enemies are everywhere. I failed to continue our family and its traditions. I failed to have children." Without hesitation, she lifted her blouse, and I saw her horribly scarred stomach.

"They even kill unborn life." Then she stared at the driver coldly. "He should have let me die that day. They found me, as they found Parvati, and claimed another life."

For a moment, tears appeared in her eyes, but she regained her composure and continued her story.

"All that is left now is to tell you why Parvati died. She died performing a sexual rite in honor of Shiva; for our family, it is a prayer to the material human body. That is all that should be cared for. What better way to honor the human body than to care for the union between man and woman and the consummation of this union. Charvaka taught us that only the material world

123

exists. Nothing in our experience tells us of the existence of God. There is no higher being responsible for our existence, so if we honor and pray, we must honor the human body. We exist through the four elements Charvaka believed in—water, fire, wind, and the earth.

"The lingam is a symbol for the original religion, before the Aryans destroyed our civilization and bent us to their morality. It is a symbol for Charvaka's ideas, suppressed by Brahman power—the enjoyment of our senses, logic, and the questioning of metaphysical nonsense. The lingam is a symbol for people who say no. We celebrate with the lingam a joining with Shiva, and we have fun doing it. Was the sex not great with Parvati? Is great sex not a spiritual truth you can adhere to?"

I found myself blushing. A twenty-year-old image of Parvati and I entwined on a chair in a brightly lit room, she on top of me, warm, sticky flesh pressed against my chest, came to my mind. I thought about her often.

"Long before the Brahman priest discovered Shiva, the Dravidians, Parvati's and my ancestors, honored his wife Shakti with elaborate rites, a live woman representing her. She was aroused to ecstatic heights to honor the goddess she personified. Centuries before the Aryans arrived on India's fertile soil we were praying to the penis of Shiva and worshipping the union of men and women. There was no guilt, no shame. It was humanity's most natural religion, with a profound cathartic flavor.

"In celebrating this union, we were hardly unique. Objects representing the sexual organs of men and women have been found all over the world. The worship of sex and the human body is as old as mankind—the oldest religion around. Uncomplicated sex worship did not last long. Soon, less invasive ways of body worship found their footing. Instead of arousing an actual woman, more contemplative forms of worship were developed. One was to worship symbols of men and women. Not long after that, the symbols became direct representations of a god, and we started praying to symbols. If you ask me, it sounds a lot less exciting than arousing a woman—or a man, for that matter.

"As old as humankind is the struggle between those who openly celebrate love in all its sexual explicitness and those who want to see sex as an expression of more esoteric love. They hide the hard penis, the wet vagina, and the bodily fluids. They do not want to see sperm in an air assault on hard-nippled breasts. It is not crude; it is human. It has always been there and always will be.

"At the base of all religion we find our sexual urges and desires for sexual union. And always, there were those teaching shame and control. We created the myth of higher human consciousness, able to celebrate love in a non-physical form. Look at Indian Tantra movements. Those of the 'right hand' school are monogamous and contemplative. There is no core of sexual gratification as a goal unto itself. The 'left hand' school has its orgies and sexual parties. Guess which school the Brahmans incorporated into Hinduism.

"Whatever path you follow, one cannot deny the spiritual force of lust and sex. Pages of great Catholic literature from monks and nuns are sexual and erotic when they talk about their love for God. The harder we try to sublimate brute sexual forces and desire and mold them into monogamous love, or a quasi-spiritual love for a deity, the faster we fail. The Taoist monk who denies himself coitus in the belief that retention of sperm will lead him to eternal life and the nuns who lock themselves away in a monastery and declare their love to God in beautifully written poems never quite take the edge off our original worship of sex. They are failed attempts to deny the hard-edged sexual nature of human beings.

"Most of us mortals just want sex and worship it in all its variety. Charvaka taught us to deal with the real world, not a perceived one, not a utopian world contrary to our perception and senses. The world is nothing; it is there to see and to be experienced. Given the choice, I'd like to see it and feel it in its most pleasure-giving form.

"Sex, and the desire for it, is ingrained at a genetic level. We wanted to follow our nature, but that was denied to us. The prudes of history try to deny us our sexual urges—the way we prayed to our gods and experienced our world. They were no match for the universal attraction of sex—for the male and female union. They were no match for Charvakian teachings—dealing with the world as it is and enjoying it while we can.

"The Brahmans never could accept our sexuality; we were living proof of Shiva's existence before the Brahman Aryans. We sent Parvati as a reminder of that to Europe, to escape the Brahman tentacles, and it was too much of a challenge to their power. She had to die and Charvaka with her. It does not seem to make sense, but the Brahmans felt that exercising power is about action and cruelty, not logic.

"I know Parvati asked you to bring these papers here, but I cannot accept them. I will leave them with you, Jan. I am the last of the family. I can do nothing with them. But do not let Charvaka die; do not let the pursuit of pleasure die. Do not let common sense, tolerance, and diversity die!"

With this, I was sent on my way. I was not up to the task. Confused, I returned to the hotel. I needed to think.

Chapter 11

Final

*J*an was an old friend. We stayed in touch over the years. He called me his best friend, but I knew this was an exaggeration, since we had not seen each other face-to-face for twenty years. I studied with him, and during our university years, we were certainly very close. I remember very clearly the day he left the house in Leuven where we lived together.

I tried to take care of him after Parvati's murder. His parents asked me to keep an eye on him. I gladly complied. But nothing could stop him from leaving soon after her death. Nothing I said could convince him to finish his studies. After he left, I did not hear from him for a couple of years. I became an editor of a major newspaper in Belgium and gained some notoriety. This is probably how Jan found me. I started receiving postcards and letters from him with friendly notes and stories of the faraway places he visited. I wrote him back, and we stayed in contact.

When I received a package with papers filled with hastily written sentences from Bangkok, I was a bit surprised to see it was from Jan. He never wrote me more than a note. Suddenly, I received a whole package of papers, bound with an elastic band and a cover letter. That letter was the first chapter of this book.

I started reading the pages Jan sent me. Some were hardly readable; I had to piece them together like a puzzle.

They covered a large part of his life, starting with Parvati's death, ending with almost delirious notes from Bangkok. When I finished reading, I thought Jan was a victim of his own imagination with his Vedic conspiracy theory, probably triggered by the dramatic events in Leuven. I thought it was a piece of bad prose.

Out of respect for my friend, I started looking into some of the details Jan had given me—the names and events mentioned and described. The accuracy of the details was partial and could be debated, but the people he talked about did exist and the events discussed were widely reported. That surprised me and made me curious.

What really disturbed me, though, were the religious overtones that permeated the story. I remembered Jan as an agnostic who had no time for people who formulated their ideas in religious terms. Religion had never had a place in his life.

The tragedy with Parvati had clearly plunged Jan into a religious merry-go-round where nothing was recognizable or what it seemed and everything was a swirl of ideas and interpretations with no beginning and no end. What made it more perplexing was that Hinduism was far from our home, geographically and culturally.

Jan recognized something common to our cultural traditions—an unshakable belief in the Holy Word. The apostles testified after Jesus' death about his life in the gospels; the rishis testified to a much older truth written down in an elaborate work that formed the spiritual base for almost a billion people. The Vedas are their direct line to eternal life and godly truths—their truth. I do not think Jan wanted to compare the content of these works or their different treatments of life and death, good and bad. What struck Jan was the fanatical belief in a book—in sentences on a piece of paper. We like to believe these writings are a direct expression of God and his will. This belief is what binds religions. In various degrees and an irrational denial of science and proof, people keep grabbing for their Bible, looking for God's will and intentions. All they ever find are words written by men with good and bad intentions, with clear consciences and sinful thoughts, with peace and murder on their minds.

Those words, depending on the efforts made to spread them, take on a life of their own, divorced from the hand that created them. By then, the damage is done. Men have to convince just one person that they are messengers from God to give the words they jotted down an irrevocable gravitas, with the power to transform societies for good, make grown men weep, and turn us against our own kind with murderous hate.

But words never express intent—not from humans, not from God. Words are signs written in black ink, surrounded by milk-white space to make them visible. Everybody owns these words and can make them speak in their own way. They are a perpetual vehicle of meaning, but they will never express the intent the original writer had when he penned them. Jan realized this; he knew anybody could read anything into anything written. If there once were something like godly intentions in the holy books, these intentions could no longer be found. People read what they want, and sometimes they read to kill or to suppress other people.

Jan was never a very sexual being. I just do not remember him like that. He had troubled relationships with women; he was dysfunctional and shy. Parvati seemed to change him. In the last months before he died, he shared stories about his sexual encounters with Parvati. They had sex with all the lights on. It was a big deal for him. He was taught to have sex in the dark, so men and women could feel each other, but not look at each other. This may seem strange, but it wasn't to me. In Catholic culture, we are taught to loathe our bodies and the desires they generate. We are taught chastity before all. As we become sexually active, we never completely shed our past, even if that past is just a reminder of what you react against.

Jan must have felt that exploring Parvati's sexually explicit beliefs was a path of liberation for him. After the initial shock of imagining Parvati in sexual rites, he must have admired her openness.

Nothing infuriates humankind more than sexuality. Despite our constant struggle to experience it in its simplicity, we seem to need to complicate, soil, restrain, and judge it with one or another holy book in hand. Nothing is more subversive than a good screw. It flaunts the veneer of culture we try to gloss onto our daily lives.

Sex is dangerous for religions because it creates an ecstasy priests want reserved for devotion to them and their gods. Sexual ecstasy reminds people of this world and its pleasures. The importance of the afterlife diminishes, and sexual union becomes the center of creation. The Brahmans must have realized that very early, as Charvaka did, and as Jan learned from Parvati and her aunt. Sexual bliss was for Charvaka and his followers a statement about the humbug the Brahman priests with their empty rituals were feeding them. Sexual ecstasy was the enjoyment of the here and now, an act of religious, social, and political resistance.

The fanatic pursuit of the Brahman priest caste for domination is hardly an isolated story. Every church in the world has created monstrous intellectual constructs to justify the killing and suppression of others. I think Jan read a bit too much into their story. He became obsessed by the Brahman conspiracy theory and believed it permeated reality on all levels, temporally and geographically. True, the Nazis were fed on Hindu dogmas. From the choice of the swastika to the Vedic concept of the superiority of the Aryan race, inspiration was found in the eternal Vedas. For all the New Age adepts out there reading and quoting Madame Blavatsky, her Theosophical Society forms a direct link between the Vedas and the National Socialist Party.

Jan realized that ideas were dangerous and multiplied uncontrollably. Good intentions have nothing to do with it. If you render your ideas to a piece of paper, you lose ownership; what happens is out of your control. You can formulate ideas with the noblest intentions, but write them down, and see how humanity perverts them. Search, and you will find that every religious text produces fanatical minds that pervert the original good intentions.

I feel Jan went even further. He seemed to believe that even writing down an idea was criminal. I do not know if I agree with this. He must have been very disappointed with life. No wonder he looked for a voice that preached enjoyment and living in the moment, skeptical laughter enjoying bodily fulfillment. I doubt, though, that Jan ever felt this enjoyment himself.

Writing these pages, I realize I put everything about Jan in the past tense, as I think he must be dead. He will never contact me again, that I know for sure. Do not ask me how I know, I just do.

He must have loved Parvati his entire life. All he wrote and all he did seemed to breathe her presence. Significant moments he talked about in his papers seemed to whisper her name. She must have been on his

134

mind every day, and all that happened to him outside his daily routine was given meaning in the light of her death. It was a tragic love story—the kind we do not find anymore. How can we? The myth of love is debunked and disgraced. I divorced three times and have children with two of my ex-wives. My life is living proof of resistance to the myth of the one soul mate the Catholic priests fed me. Life is a chain of encounters. When boredom kills joy in one relationship, the next link must be forged. Marriage as an institution died a long time ago, unless you are a very fearful human being and loneliness is your biggest fear.

I cannot but envy Jan, who had a lifelong love, a love that could only exist because Parvati was dead. Jan could picture her as his soul mate in all her majestic foreign beauty, because she was alive in his imagination. I can imagine my soul mate, not find her. And I do imagine her, and I find a lot of satisfaction in that, just as Jan must have found it satisfactory to live with the dream image of Parvati.

It is easy to dismiss everything Jan wrote as the product of a paranoid man who walked traumatized through life because of a tragedy in his youth. But does this not describe most of us? Jan made connections between significant moments in his life as he experienced them. It does not make a lot of sense, but I cannot deny some truth in his writings. He simply concocted a strange reality. I still do not understand why Parvati had to die. I read what Jan wrote, but cannot deduce why she had to be killed. Religious fanatics felt threatened in their hegemony of a truth thousands of years old, by a young woman having strange sex? It baffled me.

But religious zealots do not need much reason to react. With a holy manual in their hands, they threaten, strike fear in others, and kill. Some do good. Of course. But in light of all of this, Parvati's death is just another event in the history of religious persecution. No logic or motive need be formulated for religious zealots to obtain their goal. Try to understand them, and you wander in a world of old texts, where every quote can be countered and every point of view can be justified. People resort to force to make their view exclusive in a world of opposing ideas, but criticize any and one becomes ostracized as a sophist, a relativist, and a morally bankrupt skeptic. That is why Charvaka was killed and still dies every day.

There is not a lot of hope for us. Every day, the world becomes more wired, and ideas are readily available at the push of a button, as are all historical events and thinkers; we can construct whatever truth we want.

The cyber wave of information is a permanent assault on our senses, but this cyber wave holds thousands of untold stories and connections. We create new ones every day; some will gain notoriety, others not. Some even may become religions in their own right. We no longer learn; we are just amused—the next kick is a click away. Charvaka predicted this with his demand to reject all teachings and trust your experience.

I miss Jan and will keep his papers on Charvaka. For all his admiration of this thinker, Jan never realized that his story denounces one of the demands of Charvaka—the denunciation of inference. Without inference, Jan's story would not exist. Everything he writes is inferred. But I will keep Charvaka alive. I will drink tonight and sleep with a beautiful woman. I will sleep with her, and I will miss my troubled friend.

Pope Benedict XVI was elected in April 2005, the first elected pope of the 21th century. He declared rock and roll music evil. Let the games begin—again.